Wildwitch

Life Stealer

Wildwitch
Life Stealer

Lene Kaaberbøl

Illustrated by Rohan Eason

Translated by Charlotte Barslund

PUSHKIN CHILDREN'S BOOKS

Pushkin Press

71–75 Shelton Street

London, WC2H 9JQ

Wildwitch: Life Stealer was originally published in Danish
as *Vildheks: Kimæras hævn* by Alvilda in 2011

This translation first published by
Pushkin Children's Books in 2016

1 3 5 7 9 8 6 4 2

ISBN 978 1 782690 85 6

Set in Berling Nova by Tetragon, London

Printed and bound by CPI Group (UK) Ltd, Croydon CRO 4YY

www.pushkinpress.com

CONTENTS

CHAPTER ONE

Sparrow Heart

I was a bird. Tiny, grey-and-brown sparrow's wings carried me through the air, I darted in and out among twigs and branches, and it was spring, or nearly so. The scent of life and greenness was everywhere, and the trees had tender buds for me to eat.

Somehow I knew that I was dreaming. I knew that in real life I wasn't a sparrow, but a girl called Clara, and I definitely didn't have wings or a beak, nor would willow buds and insects be my breakfast of choice. Nevertheless I flew through that forest, sensing spring all around me, feeling the effort of moving my wings, my claws curling instinctively around delicate twigs whenever I landed to plunge my beak into a juicy bud or nip at a passing ant.

Then I spotted something on the forest floor. A berry. An orange-red, only slightly shrivelled rowanberry that no one had eaten! It was a rare treat at this time of year, and my small sparrow's tummy rumbled at the sight. Even so I didn't dive down to snatch it up at once because the berry was right next to something else, and I couldn't tell what it was. Only that it was different, that it didn't belong in a living forest. Dry leaves covered it. No, they were more than just dry, they were dead. Grey husks drained of freshness, skeletons picked clean and stripped of life.

Leaves withering and falling from the trees were nothing new. It happened every year, much to the delight of beetles, earthworms and lots of tiny, delicious, crispy bugs. This was... something else. There was no sign of insect life in the stripped leaves, nothing stirring in the deadness.

I didn't like it. But then again... I did love rowanberries. And this particular berry looked increasingly irresistible. Its juicy flesh cried "Yum!", its scent practically begged me to eat it, everything about it was so crunchy and sweet, and it had been such a long time since the last of the tasty autumn berries had been picked and eaten.

I flew down to the lowest branches. The berry was only a few wingbeats away...

Oh, oh, oh. I wanted it so much...

But I never got it.

My wings stiffened. My claws contracted a couple of times, then released their grip on the branch. I tumbled and I fell, and I couldn't unfurl my wings, I couldn't move, couldn't save myself, couldn't do a thing. My sparrow's heart pounded in my hollow chest, the blood roared through my veins, and yet... yet I couldn't move. Something had overpowered me, something invisible yet ravenous and incredibly strong; it paralysed me, squeezing the life out of me, tearing my feathers from my wings, snapping my bones like twigs. I landed on my back in the dead leaves with a thud, and the last things I saw before my eyes cracked and popped were the upside-down sky, the grey, stripped leaves and the fiery red berry I knew I would never, ever be able to reach.

"Clara!"

I flailed my arms around and hit something pointed and hard. I realized I had arms rather than wings again. I teetered on wobbly spaghetti legs, and clutched frantically at anything in reach so as not to fall. My fumbling hands closed around a handful of anorak and I clung to the coats hanging on the row of pegs outside the biology classroom at Greenacres School.

"Are you all right?" asked Oscar. "Are you ill or something? Your face looks really weird."

If it hadn't been Oscar asking, I wouldn't have said a word. But he knew practically everything there was to know. That I had an aunt who was a wildwitch, that I too was a kind of wildwitch, though not a very good one, and that ever since the day Cat had scratched my forehead and lapped up my blood with his rough, warm cat's tongue, my life had been turned upside down.

"I was a bird," I burst out. "I was flying around being a bird, but then... I died."

Someone giggled behind me. Josefine. Well, it would be her, wouldn't it? When it came to sheer bitchiness, she held the class record.

"Clara thinks she's turned herself into a bird," she announced loudly. "I don't think the spell worked, though. Why don't you flap your wings so we can see?"

I was too shattered to ignore her or hit her with a witty comeback, though I knew it would be the smart thing to do. My heart was pounding just as hard as the sparrow's, and I found myself touching my eyelids to check that the eyeballs underneath were normal, round and intact under the soft skin, and not squashed like a berry someone had stepped on. What *was* that thing that had killed the sparrow?

And why – why and how was it possible for me to be dreaming when I was wide awake? One minute I'd been outside my classroom with Oscar, the next...

"Clara." Oscar touched my arm. "Do you want me to go get a teacher?"

"No. No, I'm OK. I... I was just daydreaming."

He could tell that it was a lie, but he didn't say anything. It was his fault that the others had started teasing me, and this time not just about us snogging – we weren't, just each other's best friends – but about me being a witch. Or to be precise, because they thought that I *believed* I was a witch and could do all sorts of magic tricks. Oscar had told Alex from his class, and everyone knew that Alex couldn't keep a secret any longer than he could hold his breath, so now it was all over the school. Except, of course, that no one had the faintest clue what it really meant to be a wildwitch, nor would they ever understand what a wildwitch could and couldn't do.

Right now, apparently, I couldn't walk from one classroom to the next without turning into a bird. Not quite the perfect start to my day.

"You go on," I said to Oscar because I knew he had a music lesson coming up. "I'll see you later."

He glanced over his shoulder – twice – as he walked off, but in the end he did leave. He was only too aware that we mustn't act too weird. Not after Oscar had gone missing for two whole days because Chimera had abducted him. Oscar's mum still believed that we'd been mixed up in some kind of fantasy role-play, and she thought being with me "undermined his grasp of reality," as she put it. She would prefer us not to hang out too much, and she'd started sending poor Oscar to some therapist every other Wednesday.

I leaned surreptitiously against the wall and tried to pretend that nothing had happened. Josefine was just bursting to tell more jokes at my expense and was already busy entertaining her friend Ina with stories about birds and wings and Clara's weird ideas.

So I *tried* to pretend, but really I felt both sad and scared. Sad because... because although it had just been a dream, it had felt so real. The sparrow's heart had broken, the little bird had died. And I couldn't help but mourn it.

Scared, because... well, because I've never had a dream while standing up before. And what if? What if the dream... wasn't a dream? What if it were real?

CHAPTER TWO

Badgers and Other Beasts

Spring was on its way – not just in the forest of my dream sparrow, but also in the real world. Forsythia glowed yellow against the shower-spattered walls of the houses, and sunbeams bounced off the puddles on the gravel paths in Jupiter Park. I was sitting on a damp bench while Oscar dutifully plodded around with Woofer, his black labrador, following Woofer's usual peeing route. Cat was lounging on the bench next to me, watching the dog with every sign of superior contempt.

"Cat?" I whispered.

What?

His answer came lazy and rather languid. Sometimes his voice inside my head sounds as if he's spent his whole life lying on a silk cushion, lapping up cream; at other times it's so rough and gruff you'd think he was the biggest, baddest alley cat ever to claw a rival in a dustbin fight. Today it was the silk cushion voice.

"I think... I think I need to speak to Aunt Isa." The sparrow had been on my mind all day. Not all the time, lots of other things had happened, lessons and lunch and breaks and chatting about normal stuff, but in-between. Any time I wasn't specifically thinking of something else, in fact.

Cat didn't ask why. Instead he jumped onto my lap and sniffed my chin, my nose, my eyes and my head. Then he sat down on his wide, muscly rear end and planted his right front paw on my shoulder. Very carefully and without claws, he placed his left paw between my eyebrows, in the exact same spot where six months ago he'd given me the claw marks that had since faded into pale, practically invisible scars.

"What are you doing?" I asked nervously.

He made no reply. And nothing happened, not really. Nothing except me remembering what it was like to be the sparrow at the moment of its death. Which was quite enough. My whole body trembled and my hand shot up to my heart, while the other tried to protect my eyes.

Cat hissed and bristled. He was already big, practically as big as Woofer, but when he raised his fur like that, he grew simply enormous. His golden eyes flashed.

Come, he said.

"Now? But..."

Now.

"But... Oscar. Mum. At least let me..." But you can't argue with Cat. He doesn't understand about being back when you promised your mum you would be, or telling people where you're going. Or he does understand, but he just doesn't care.

He sprang down onto the path in a supple feline leap, and I lost sight of Oscar, the forsythia and the buildings around the park. Everything disappeared in dense fog, which meant we were already on the wildways, though I could still feel the bench underneath me.

"Cat! No!"

Come. Now.

My protests were completely useless. If I'd been a proper wildwitch, I would have been able to decide if I wanted to travel the wildways *and* I would have been able to do it alone. But for the time being, I couldn't even find my way to Aunt Isa's without help, and if Cat said *now*, then now it was.

It only took a moment. Although Aunt Isa lived about as far off the beaten track as it was possible to get – it took hours and hours on very poor roads if you went by car – I barely had time to write a rushed text message to Oscar before we'd arrived.

"Clara! Clara, look! I can flyyyyyyyyyyyy!"

A ruffled bundle of feathers flapped through the air before crashing into my shoulder.

"Oops. Sorry," said a breathless Nothing. "I'm... not so good... at the landing bit yet."

The Nothing was about the size of an owl with grey-and-brown feathers and short, stumpy wings, but she had human hands instead of talons, and a lost little girl's face where you would expect to see a beak and predatory eyes. Chimera had made her – The Nothing called her "Mum" and that was partly true – but in Chimera's opinion, she was a failure and so utterly useless that she didn't deserve a name other than The Nothing. She'd spent most of her life in a cage because Chimera had got fed up with The Nothing following her around all the time. She couldn't groom her own feathers and, because she was allergic to dust mites, she often sneezed and her eyes tended to water. Or they used to.

"Wow, you look great!" I burst out, which was true, even though The Nothing was at that particular moment sitting on her rump in the wet grass, clumsily batting her wings to get back on an even keel.

"You think so?" she said. "Really?"

"Yes." Her feathers were glossy and immaculately groomed, and the permanent trails of snots and tears that used to stain her chest had gone. "And you can fly!"

"Yes!" She flapped her wings even harder and raised herself a short distance off the ground. "I still... get very... puffed out, but I'm... getting better."

Bumble came galloping across the farmyard, barking and wagging his tail and acting as if my turning up was the best thing that had ever happened to him. Aunt Isa followed, more slowly and not quite as hyper, but she gave me a warm smile.

"Clara! What a surprise. Does your mum know you're here?"

"Eh... no. It was a spur of the moment thing."

"Has something happened?"

I shook my head. "I'm not sure. It... it was a kind of dream. But a really weird one. And Cat thought it couldn't wait."

Aunt Isa narrowed her eyes and looked at Cat.

"Why not?" she said, and she was asking Cat. But Cat just swished his tail a couple of times and looked silent and very feline.

Aunt Isa pressed her lips together. "Hm," she

said. "I guess that's what you get for having a cat as your wildfriend. They go their own ways. Well, come on in. We can call your mum later."

There was practically no mobile coverage where Aunt Isa lived – you had to walk to the top of the hill behind the farmhouse and the barn to get a signal. Her house was sort of in a world of its own, in a valley with a meadow and a brook, nestled between wooded hills, dark with spruce, and russet and brown with bracken and leafless beeches.

On the stone steps, there were bowls of cat food set out for hungry newly awakened hedgehogs, home-made suet and seed balls were hanging from the apple trees, and there were feeders everywhere for every imaginable kind of bird, plus no doubt a few I'd never heard of. A couple of mallards waddled around the farmyard, grubbing in the puddles, taking little notice of Bumble or Cat. Nor did they have any reason to. Bumble was too good-natured and too polite to do them any harm, and Cat regarded attacking a duck as beneath his dignity. From the barn I could hear a sleepy chiiirp from Hoot-Hoot, Aunt Isa's owl, probably perched on one of the beams trying to get a good day's sleep.

I followed Aunt Isa into the hallway, hung my down jacket on the coat rack, and kicked off my boots. Then I noticed another pair, quite familiar-looking.

"Is Kahla here?" I asked. Kahla was Aunt Isa's wildwitch apprentice and came for lessons most days of the week.

"Yes," my aunt said. "But she's busy working on an assignment, so don't talk to her until she talks to you."

Kahla, it turned out, was sitting at the big work-table in the living room, wrapped in seven or eight colourful garments, as usual, with a stripy hat covering her jet-black hair even though she was indoors. Her eyes were closed, but in her hand she held a pencil, which moved jerkily across a drawing pad lying open in front of her.

I hadn't seen her for a long time. I guess we were friends of sorts, although we hadn't exactly hit it off last autumn when Aunt Isa started teaching me a couple of basic wildwitch survival skills. Kahla was very advanced. She could do everything I couldn't, and it was hard not to be jealous when everything I struggled and failed at was clearly a walk in the park to her. Nor had she tried to hide her irritation at having a newbie on the team. However, she'd come to my rescue when I really needed it, and since then things had improved.

It felt a bit weird to walk past her without even saying hi, but I genuinely don't think she noticed us. Apart from her hand holding the pencil, she was sitting so still she could have been a garden gnome.

"What's she doing?" I whispered to Aunt Isa.

"You don't have to whisper," she replied. "Just don't say her name because it might distract her. She's Journeying. She borrows the eyes and the ears of any animal willing to act as her host."

"I thought you had to..." I touched the scars on my forehead where Cat had scratched me and licked my blood so that we'd be able to communicate.

"... I mean, that you needed blood."

"Blood binds. It creates a connection that can't be severed. This is different. She's just a guest, a stranger visiting for as long as the animal is willing to invite her in. When she leaves it, there will be no ties left over, possibly not even a memory that she was ever there."

I noticed how much care Aunt Isa took not to say Kahla's name. Bumble, too, left her alone, and The Nothing flapped around her in a wide, wobbly arc before landing clumsily on one of the threadbare armchairs.

"Pheeewww..." she said. "Flying is hard work!"

Bumble climbed up on the sofa with familiar ease. He did have a basket, but he rarely used it. Besides, it currently had another occupant, one with a flat, black-and-white head and a broad, grey back.

"Is that a badger?" I asked.

"Yes," Aunt Isa said. "She was hit by a car and broke her hip. It's almost healed now, but she still can't look after herself very well, and she's due to give birth soon."

Most badgers looked rather squat to me, but I realized this one was rather broader than usual. She gave me a surly look and curled up, protecting her big belly. To her, I was clearly an unwelcome intruder.

"They're nocturnal, of course," Aunt Isa said a tad apologetically. "They prefer peace and quiet during the day so they can sleep. But why don't you sit down and tell me why you're here."

I squeezed myself onto the sofa next to Bumble and told her about my sparrow dream. Aunt Isa listened without interrupting.

"So what was that all about?" I asked.

Aunt Isa glanced sideways at Kahla, who was still lost to the world.

"It's odd, but it sounds almost like you were Journeying too," she said. "As if you accidentally got the sparrow to host you."

"Are you... are you saying that it was *real*? Not a dream?"

"It's possible."

I felt a sudden chill in my stomach and in my heart. Small animals died all the time, I knew that. Big animals ate smaller ones, and I had to accept that part of nature, if I wanted to be a wildwitch. But this was different.

"Aunt Isa...?"

"Yes?"

"Well... if it really happened, then... what do you think killed the sparrow?" Bones snapping so easily, the heart and eyes being squeezed until they burst and yet the killer was invisible to the sparrow, unseen and without sound or scent.

"I don't know," Aunt Isa said. "But I think we had better find out."

CHAPTER THREE

Flying High

"Lie down and relax," Aunt Isa said. "You're not used to this, and this way there's a limit to how far you can fall... "

I lay down on the floor in Aunt Isa's living room like a good girl. Cat immediately settled on top of me, on my legs and my tummy, and sank his claws into my jumper. The message was clear: I wasn't going anywhere without him. This suited me just fine. His wilfulness meant he wasn't the perfect bodyguard, but he was fiercely protective of me when he did show up. And I was nowhere near as relaxed as Aunt Isa wanted me to be.

Kahla had returned from her own Journeying. On the pad she had sketched and drawn some of the things she had seen while she had had her eyes closed: a strange landscape of deep, dark valleys and towering, golden-brown columns, which turned out to be how a pine cone looks when you're a beetle, a wren's eye view through a mesh of twigs and branches and huge, withered beech leaves, and a wet forest of earthworm-smelling grass as seen by a hedgehog. Aunt Isa had nodded and praised her and asked her to tell us everything she had experienced. I don't think she did it just to check Kahla's work, but also to encourage and reassure me. Journeying could be exciting, different, fun even... you could tell from the glow in Kahla's eyes as she spoke. But my involuntary Journeying – if that really was what it had been – had ended with the death of the sparrow. I didn't fancy another go. Especially not when the aim was to return to the spot where the sparrow had fallen.

"Please try to relax," Aunt Isa instructed me for the umpteenth time half an hour later.

"I *am* relaxed," I said through gritted teeth.

"No, you're not, sweetheart," she said with a wry smile. "Here you go. Let's see if some valerian tea might help."

I pulled a face. Aunt Isa's valerian tea tended to be quite bitter, but I took the cup anyway.

"I put in two teaspoons of dried valerian," The Nothing piped up eagerly, "from the small blue caddy next to the camomile tea. I'm starting to know where everything is."

I lay down again. The valerian tea made my lips tingle, and I did actually begin to relax. Then again, it might also have been that by now I was convinced nothing was going to happen. I was prepared to accept that Kahla could zoom around pretending to be a beetle, a hedgehog or a wren, but I clearly couldn't. At least, not deliberately. I yawned. Nope, it didn't feel like anything was going to happen today.

I dreamed I was on a swing. Higher and higher, wilder and wilder. The ropes burned my palms, but I didn't care. When I leaned back and kicked out my legs to go faster, I flung back my head so that I was looking right up at a landscape of white clouds and blue, blue sky and only a little bit of the treetop I couldn't quite get rid of.

"Be careful!" my younger sister called out. "Don't go so high!"

I didn't have a younger sister, or indeed any sisters. But I seemed to have one in the dream.

I ignored her. I wanted to go higher, to let go of the ground, let go of the ropes and fly off. I wanted to be a bird, so that I could fly far, far away.

When the swing was at its highest point, I jumped. The sky was so blue, the wind was in my hair; if I were ever going to fly, this was my chance.

I flew. For one brilliantly wild, blue moment.

Then I hit the ground so hard it felt as if every bone in my body must break.

"Kimmie!"

I could hear the terror in her voice, but I ignored her. I lay very still and tried hard not to breathe. I could have stood up – I'd known almost immediately that I wasn't seriously hurt. But I continued to lie very still.

"Kimmie. Please sit up."

My sister touched me, first tentatively, then more impatiently. "Kimmie!"

I'm dead, I thought. I'm not here any more. I'm a white cloud in the blue, blue sky, and now I'm drifting away.

I could hear sniffling.

"You're not really dead," she said. "Are you?"

Yet still I held my breath and didn't move a muscle.

She started to cry properly.

"Mum!" she cried out. "Muuuuum..." Now stammering because she was running – I could hear her footsteps. And I could tell from her voice that she was panicking.

"Wait!" I rolled onto one side. "Come back. I'm all right..."

It took a long time to calm her down. "I thought you were dead," she kept saying. "I thought you were dead..."

"Clara!"

Aunt Isa was calling me.

"What?" I said.

"I think you dozed off. Maybe just the one teaspoon of valerian tea next time."

"Did you have any dreams?" Kahla asked. "Anything about animals?"

"No," I said. "Just something about two girls and a swing."

"That doesn't sound like Journeying."

"No," I said. "So I guess it wasn't."

I half sat up. I could almost feel Kahla's eyes boring into the back of my neck. She'd been helpful today and not patronizing in the least, but somehow that only made it worse. Now I couldn't even get mad at her – only at myself.

Why was I such a rubbish wildwitch? If I was destined to be one, then why was it so hard? Given that it had turned my life upside down and messed with my head, upset my mum, made the other kids at school tease me – then couldn't I at least be good at it? Like Kahla was.

Cat got up and arched his back – still on top of me and with all four paws on my tummy. And he wasn't a lightweight cat.

"Get off," I told him. "I can't breathe."

He sent me a look I couldn't decipher. Then slowly and leisurely he stepped onto the floor, one paw at a time. Not exactly instant obedience, but at least he did shift himself.

"Are you upset?" asked The Nothing from her armchair. She was sitting with her finger-feet stretched out in front of her with a notebook in one foot and a pencil in the other, ready to write down anything exciting that might happen during my Journeying. Needless to say, the page was blank.

"No," I said. "Just... fed up."

"I'm pretty useless too," she said and sneezed sadly. "But... I do practise."

It was heartbreaking. Even The Nothing was better than me because she didn't give up – she kept on trying. I got up so suddenly that the badger growled at me from the dog basket.

"Where are you going?" Aunt Isa asked.

"Home."

She studied me for a little while.

"Yes," she then said. "It's probably for the best. We don't want your mum to get too worried. But I think you should come back tomorrow. We could have another go."

"Mum wouldn't like it."

"No, I know. Has she told you not to visit me?"

I shook my head. "Not in so many words."

CHAPTER FOUR

A Snake in the Grass

"Hi, Mousie. Where have you been?"

"With Oscar." Would it be wise to leave it at that? Not to mention Aunt Isa? We never did get round to calling Mum and, besides, I was home now, wasn't I? I was sorely tempted to keep quiet because I knew telling her would upset her. My mum's worst nightmare had pretty much come true that day about six months ago when Cat came into my life. Mum had never told me about Aunt Isa, as a matter of fact, I might not even have known I had an aunt, except that we would sometimes see her exceptionally lifelike animal illustrations on cards, in books, or on mugs or napkins. That was how she earned her living – she was a highly skilled artist with the added advantage that she could persuade most animals to "sit" for her whenever she needed them to. But the other stuff – the fact that she was a wildwitch – I would probably never have known at all if it hadn't been for Cat scratching my forehead and forcing my mum to take me to Aunt Isa's so that I could learn enough not to be in mortal danger most of the time.

My mum desperately wanted me to be normal. She wanted us to carry on living as we always had and for Aunt Isa, Cat and all of the wildworld to just leave us alone. Nature terrified her and she was always scared that something would happen to me.

But we'd reached a compromise. Mostly thanks to my dad, who had convinced her that it would be foolish to ban me from visiting my own aunt. So I was allowed to visit Aunt Isa, only I had to tell Mum where I was going. No lying, no disappearing. That was the deal.

"Erm... and then I just stopped by to visit Aunt Isa."

Mum looked up and forgot all about the carrot she was peeling.

"Oh," she said and made a real effort to pretend that she was cool with that. "And how was Isa?"

"Great," I said. "She's looking after a badger. It's going to have babies soon."

"Is that right? Well, that'll be nice."

It was almost worse than her being mad at me. If she'd screamed and shouted, I could have reminded her of our agreement, and that would have meant I was in the right. Now she just stood there smiling, while at the same time I could see how upset she really was. Whenever she looked like that I felt all prickly and itchy on the inside and I desperately wanted it to stop and for her to be happy instead.

"So will you be going back to help out with the badger cubs?" she asked carefully. She was trying to look relaxed, but one hand was clenched tightly on the carrot and the other around the peeler, and she hadn't started peeling again. The tap was running, and she just stood there, her hands trembling slightly.

"Maybe." Scratch, itch. The horrid feeling inside me got stronger. "Or... no. I don't think so. I don't think the badger likes me much."

"Is that so," Mum said and her smile became a little more genuine. "Then again, badgers tend to be quite bad-tempered."

The horridness inside me began to ease. I took a deep breath and the prickling sensation went away.

"What's for dinner?" I asked.

"Lasagne," she said. "Would you like to give me a hand?"

I took a knife from the drawer and together we prepared the salad. Then the timer went off and I put on thick, padded oven gloves to get the lasagne out of the oven. It was boiling hot and thick bubbles rose in the cheese sauce and burst lazily like burps of gas in molten lava.

"Mind how you go, Mousie," Mum said.

"Yeah, sure."

The steam from the lasagne danced in the air in front of me. I was standing in the middle of the floor with the piping hot dish in my hands, and suddenly I couldn't take my eyes off the steam. There was something inside it, something less transparent than the rest of it. A foggy thread, fat and grey. A stripped leaf. A sparrow's carcass picked clean and crushed. I had no hands any more, no legs either. I slithered across the ground feeling the moist leaves against my belly, sticking out my tongue to smell better... Yes, there were a few fibres of meat on that skeleton, not many, but I was hungry, my body was still sluggish from hibernation, and even though a living mouse would have been preferable, a dead sparrow was still food.

"No," I whispered.

But the grass snake didn't listen. Hunger gnawed its belly and it was oblivious to the death zone on the forest floor.

"Clara! Watch what you're doing with that dish!"

I gasped for air. The dish slipped between my fingers, it was strange suddenly to have hands again, they didn't feel as though they were mine.

"Clara!"

The lasagne tipped, tumbled and fell. Cheese and hot meat sauce splashed over my tummy and legs, burning, and instantly snapping me out of my strange snakeness and back to myself.

"Ouch..."

"Mousie! Trousers off. Now!"

I just stood there with the oven gloves on my outstretched hands and in the end my mum had to peel the sauce-stained trousers off me. The skin underneath was speckled and red.

"Get into the shower and turn on the cold tap now," my mum ordered me. "Clara, come on. Wake up!"

She made me aim the showerhead at my legs for more than a quarter of an hour. My skin still stung and the largest of the red splodges refused to go away completely, but it eased the pain. Mum applied a burns ointment and that helped even more.

"The lasagne..." I began.

"Never mind about the lasagne," Mum said gruffly.

"But what about dinner?"

"Are you hungry, sweetheart?"

"Yes. A bit." A lot, if truth be told. As if the grass snake's end-of-winter hunger still rumbled in my tummy.

She smiled. "Well, I guess that means you're on the mend. We'll order a pizza. After all, we still have the salad..."

CHAPTER FIVE

The Scent of Blood

"So... did you turn into an actual grass snake?" Oscar asked me the next day after I'd tried to explain.

"No," I said. "It just felt like I did. Totally weird. No arms, no legs, just wiggling on my belly..."

"Cool," he said. "I'd love to have a go at that..."

I shuddered for a moment. "No, you wouldn't," I said. "Especially not in... in that place, trust me."

"Why's that?"

"Because something's wrong there. It's like there's a... a death zone. And any animal that comes near it dies."

"So the grass snake is dead?"

"I don't know. I dropped the lasagne before I reached the death zone. Or... before the grass snake did."

"But you think it's dead?"

I rubbed my arm. The goose pimples refused to go away.

"It was just like with the sparrow. Exactly like it. And Aunt Isa says it's not just a dream."

The school playground was filled with screaming kids. Normally I took no notice of the mayhem, but today it somehow sounded louder than usual, the light was sharper, and the spring air seemed to affect my skin, my poor naked human skin, unprotected by fur, feathers or scales.

"Still, I really wish I could do that... What did you call it again?"

"Journeying."

"Yeah, that Journeying thing. You don't know how lucky you are."

I didn't feel lucky at all and I couldn't understand why he couldn't see how utterly revolting it was.

"It's not like I decide to do it," I said. "It... it just takes me over. I still have burns on my legs from the lasagne."

That seemed to get through to him.

"Oh. Well, that's obviously not cool. And just think what could have happened if you'd been on your bike? And a bus or something had come along. Splat!"

I pulled a face.

"Cut it out, will you?" I said.

"Yeah, all right. Just saying."

"And I wish you wouldn't."

38

"Clara, if you don't mind my saying so... you're in a bit of a mood today."

I stopped in the middle of the playground, folded my arms across my chest and did my best to stare him down.

"A bit of a mood?" I said.

"Yeah. Just saying. Maybe it's a girl thing."

"Fancy being turned into a grass snake?" I said. "I could always have a word with Aunt Isa."

He didn't even bat an eyelid.

"Would you?" he sounded thrilled. "That would be awesome!"

I gave up.

"You're a lost cause," I said, and headed for the bike shed.

A bunch of kids had gathered there, some from my own class, some from Oscar's, but rather than head home or make their way to the after-school club, they were huddled in giggling pairs or small clusters, so it didn't take a genius to work out that they were up to something.

I zigzagged through the crowd to the bike racks. The new, pale-blue, five-gear bicycle I'd been given for Christmas was gone. Where I'd parked it, there was now a broom. One of those old-fashioned brooms with a bunch of birch twigs tied around a stick. It looked a bit makeshift.

"I thought you said you were in a hur
home?" Josefine quipped. "This should
easier and faster..."

The giggling was no longer muted and s
by now most people were laughing their l

My cheeks turned hot.

"Yes, all right, very funny," I said. "H
Now where's my bike?"

"How about a lap of honour?" It was Marc
to be witty. "I've never seen a witch fly b

"Leave her alone," Oscar said. "It's not

"Please may I have my bike. Now." I t
hard to handle the situation politely, but
easy.

And then I started feeling something
sensation in my body, a rustling of feath
strong talons flexing...

No!

With great effort, I managed to shak
whatever it was. Not now. Not here. In
anywhere, ever.

At that moment, someone grabbed
behind and lifted me up so my feet wer
ground.

"Stop it. Put me down!"

They didn't. Instead other hands gra
flailing arms from above and pulled me ev

"Clara, if you don't mind my saying so... you're in a bit of a mood today."

I stopped in the middle of the playground, folded my arms across my chest and did my best to stare him down.

"A bit of a mood?" I said.

"Yeah. Just saying. Maybe it's a girl thing."

"Fancy being turned into a grass snake?" I said. "I could always have a word with Aunt Isa."

He didn't even bat an eyelid.

"Would you?" he sounded thrilled. "That would be awesome!"

I gave up.

"You're a lost cause," I said, and headed for the bike shed.

A bunch of kids had gathered there, some from my own class, some from Oscar's, but rather than head home or make their way to the after-school club, they were huddled in giggling pairs or small clusters, so it didn't take a genius to work out that they were up to something.

I zigzagged through the crowd to the bike racks. The new, pale blue, five-gear bicycle I'd been given for Christmas was gone. Where I'd parked it, there was now a broom. One of those old-fashioned brooms with a bunch of birch twigs tied around a stick. It looked a bit makeshift.

"I thought you said you were in a hurry to get home?" Josefine quipped. "This should make it easier and faster..."

The giggling was no longer muted and scattered, by now most people were laughing their heads off.

My cheeks turned hot.

"Yes, all right, very funny," I said. "Ha-ha-ha. Now where's my bike?"

"How about a lap of honour?" It was Marcus trying to be witty. "I've never seen a witch fly before!"

"Leave her alone," Oscar said. "It's not funny."

"Please may I have my bike. Now." I tried very hard to handle the situation politely, but it wasn't easy.

And then I started feeling something again – a sensation in my body, a rustling of feathers, long, strong talons flexing...

No!

With great effort, I managed to shake it off... whatever it was. Not now. Not here. In fact, not anywhere, ever.

At that moment, someone grabbed me from behind and lifted me up so my feet were off the ground.

"Stop it. Put me down!"

They didn't. Instead other hands grabbed my flailing arms from above and pulled me even higher into the air. I felt something give in my shoulder and I wiggled madly to escape. "She just needs a leg up," said another voice, deeper and hoarser than Marcus's or the other boys from my year. I craned my neck, but whoever was holding my arms was sitting on the roof of the bike shed, and I couldn't see him properly. Even so, I already knew who it was. Martin the Meanie. Martin the Meanie from Year 10.

Marcus stared at me with his mouth open.

"Eh..." he stuttered.

"Get me the broomstick," Martin ordered him. "Let's see if she can really fly!"

I couldn't keep it at bay any longer. The playground disappeared, woods opened up beneath me and the red scent of fresh blood drowned out everything else. The prey in my talons continued to struggle, its long, red squirrel tail flicking from side to side so that I had to stiffen my wings against the updraught. I scouted for a landing spot, so that I could plunge my beak into its warm flesh and assuage my hunger. There, a bare spot, a tree with naked branches...

No!

I tried to free myself from the wings, the hunger and the blood. Out. Away. Home. The bird plummeted without warning and I plummeted with it, unable to control anything, unable to hold on to anything.

No. No!

The squirrel's body slipped from my talons. I screamed. The squirrel squealed. Suddenly there were shrill cries all around us, and the ground came hurtling towards me, dead, wrong; I let go of the prey and saw it fall towards the death zone while at the last minute I found my wings again, straightening, soaring, flapping and flying, without my prey, but at least I was alive.

The shrill voices did not go away.

And I wasn't flying anywhere either. I was lying on the ground, staring up at the sky, hearing Josefine sob hysterically, while Marcus's ashen face, his mouth a very big, round, shocked O, swam into focus somewhere above me.

"Get a teacher!" someone called out.

"We don't need a teacher," Oscar said through gritted teeth; he was pressing buttons on his mobile. "We need an ambulance."

I felt well enough to speak and thought that I would be able to stand up in a minute; I was fairly sure of it.

"I think..." I gasped, "I don't think that... I need..." Ambulance, hospital, all of that. "Not necessary..."

"Not for you," Oscar said. "For him."

It was only then that I realized that someone was lying next to me. Martin. Very flat, very still. And all I could think of was the way he smelt. Of fresh blood – just like the squirrel.

CHAPTER SIX

Blue-Light

The paramedics had insisted on putting me on
a stretcher even though I felt perfectly capable of
sitting up and walking without help.

Martin, however, couldn't.

He lay limply on the other stretcher in the
ambulance, his breathing heavy and rattling, and
the whole of one side of his black jacket was torn
and gleaming wetly.

"He's losing blood," one of the paramedics
said.

"Cut off his jacket," said the ambulance doctor
who was holding an oxygen mask over Martin's
nose and mouth with one hand while pulling back
Martin's eyelids with the other. He let go of the
oxygen mask and shone a small pocket torch into
Martin's eyes. "I need his blood pressure!"

They were so busy with Martin that I felt massively in the way, but then again, I hadn't forced

them to take me in the ambulance. I lay as still as a mouse, trying not to disturb anyone.

"How did he get those cuts?" the doctor wanted to know.

"There was a tree beside the bike shed," the paramedic said. "Perhaps some of the branches... then again, his jacket isn't ripped in the same place."

"Martin. Martin!" The doctor patted Martin's cheek so hard that it was almost a slap. "Can you hear me?"

But Martin couldn't.

"He's not responding," the doctor said. "I want him scanned as soon as we get to the hospital."

"Are we blue-lighting him?" the paramedic asked.

"Yes, we are."

The paramedic told the driver and seconds later the howl of sirens cut through the noise of the traffic, and I felt the smooth surge as the ambulance accelerated.

They wheeled Martin away as soon as we reached the hospital, and the last I saw of him was a glimpse of his pale, bluish face under the oxygen mask as they pushed the gurney out of the ambulance.

"You just wait there," one of the paramedics called to me over his shoulder, "someone will be with you in a minute."

And someone was. A man dressed in green with a moustache and tired but friendly eyes who was wearing a badge announcing in capital letters that his name was ERIC HANSEN and that he was a PORTER.

"Hiya," he said. "You're Clara, aren't you? I believe I'm taking you to A&E. I hear you fell off a roof, is that right?"

"Yes, or... almost. But I don't think I'm hurt..."

"How do you almost fall off a roof?" he asked with a twinkle in his eyes. "Did you change your mind half-way?"

"No. I mean... I hadn't quite reached the roof when we fell. Do you know what's happened to Martin? Is he... is he badly hurt?"

"The doctor's with him now," he said. "They're taking good care of him."

That didn't make me any the wiser and besides, it felt a bit weird to have a conversation while I was lying flat on my back and being rolled down a hospital corridor.

"I can actually walk on my own," I tried again.

"Yes, I certainly hope so," said ERIC HANSEN, PORTER. "But just to be on the safe side, they'll probably want to X-ray your back before you start jumping about again. It's standard procedure for people who almost fall off roofs."

"**Y**ou're just a touch concussed, I think," the A&E doctor said. "So it's best if you lie here until your mum comes to fetch you. Do you feel nauseous?"

"No. I just feel a bit... strange."

"That sounds about right." She smiled and gave my arm a quick pat. "You need to take it easy for the next couple of days, do you understand? No climbing on roofs for at least a week or so. And if reading or watching television gives you a headache, then stop."

"OK." I was getting fed up with explaining that I hadn't actually been on the blasted roof. "How's Martin?"

"Is he your friend?"

No, that would be a lie.

"We go to the same school," I said.

"Another doctor is with him now," she said, almost like the porter. And then she went off to deal with the next unfortunate case in the A&E queue.

By now I was in a hospital bed, but luckily I was still wearing my own clothes. I was glad they weren't keeping me in overnight because I'd much rather be back in my own bed, in my own room. I actually felt worse now than in the moments following the fall, or maybe I was just starting to feel it more. And it wasn't just getting knocked on the head that was the problem.

I absolutely had to find out what had happened to Martin. How did he get those cuts? Why had I thought he smelled of squirrel blood? And why did we fall?

I sat up gingerly. My head would definitely prefer me to be lying down, but I was only slightly dizzy and the X-ray doctor had assured me that my back was totally fine. I wished I was home. I wished that Cat was here. I usually felt stronger and braver when Cat was nearby.

Of course.

A black, furry figure emerged from the shadowy darkness under my bed.

"Cat!"

I was so pleased to see him that I couldn't help pulling him up on my lap and hugging him. He hissed at me and placed a warning claw on my bare arm. He was nobody's cuddly toy.

Come.

He leapt down easily onto the pale blue linoleum.

"Where are we going?"

We're going to find the one who smells of squirrel.

"Martin? But... they won't tell me anything. I've asked twenty times, at least. They just keep saying 'the doctor's taking care of him'. I don't know where he is!"

Use your nose, Cat said, as if it were the most obvious thing in the world. *How hard can it be to find a squirrel in a hospital?*

CHAPTER SEVEN

Falling Hard

Martin was in somewhere called Intensive Care. The room had no windows and an insane number of machines monitored and measured this, that and the other while beeping quietly to themselves. It was hot and a bit stuffy and only a thin sheet covered Martin's legs and lower body. His arms and his big, red hands lay far too nicely and neatly alongside his body; it didn't look natural. And his hands weren't even that red any more, but pale and spotted like the underside of a plaice, and plastered with tubes and cannulas.

He really did smell of squirrel. And quite strongly of blood. I could feel my nostrils flare involuntarily, as if I were a rabbit. How could I possibly smell that? And how had Martin ended up smelling of squirrel when there hadn't been one for miles around, at least not in the real world?

He was with you, Cat replied instantly. *You took him with you on your Journeying. And then you dropped him.*

I looked down at Cat. The golden eyes in his broad face stared up unblinkingly. I didn't know what to say because no matter how far-fetched it sounded, I worried that he might be right. It felt like he was.

"Oi. No animals allowed in here!"

I turned around. A young man in a nurse's uniform was making his way towards me from a glass cubicle across the corridor.

"Animals?" I said innocently, while at the same time sending Cat a very firm and determined "get lost" thought. "Where?"

The male nurse stopped. He bent down to look under Martin's bed, but to no avail. All that was left of Cat was a splodge of wildways fog that was already dispersing.

"I thought I saw... there was a cat in here, wasn't there?"

"In here? How would it have got in?"

"No," he said. "I guess you're right. Anyway, children aren't allowed either. Not unless they have permission."

"Sorry," I said. "It's just... no one would tell me how he was."

"Who?"

"Martin." I pointed – I couldn't remember his surname. "We're at school together."

His gaze softened and became more sympathetic.

"Are you a friend of his?" he asked.

"Yes," I lied.

"You can sit with him for a while if you like," the nurse said. "But don't touch anything."

"Erm... thanks."

I didn't think I could leave now, so I sat down on a grey plastic chair next to the bed.

"Talk to him. He might be able to hear you."

"Oh... OK. I'll give it a go."

The nurse tilted his head slightly and studied me.

"Were you the girl who fell with him?" he asked.

I blushed. I could actually feel the heat spreading across my face.

"Yes."

"How far was it from the roof?"

"Not very. It was only a bike shed."

"Yes, so we were told. Only he wasn't as lucky as you."

"What's happened to him?"

"He hit his head quite hard, he cracked a shoulder blade and broke two ribs. And we had to suture

52

some lacerations." He looked at me. "It takes quite a lot to break a shoulder blade," he said. "That's why I've been thinking... that you'd really think he had fallen from something higher up."

I thought about wings and beaks and talons. And about the squirrel's small, maimed body tumbling, falling through the air. Much further than the distance from the roof of an old bike shed.

Then I heard tentative footsteps from the corridor. An old woman in a drenched, beige winter coat came in. She was wearing a knitted white hat and matching woollen gloves, and she was clutching a brown handbag with both hands.

"Excuse me," she said. "I'm looking for my grandson..." Then she spotted Martin and stopped in her tracks.

"Mrs Winter?" The nurse asked. "You're Martin's grandmother, aren't you?"

"Yes," she said. "They told me... he'd had a fall... he... it's not serious, is it?"

"Take a seat, Mrs Winter. The doctor will be with you shortly. We also have some papers for you to sign. You're Martin's guardian, aren't you?"

"He lives with me," she said absent-mindedly, never once taking her eyes off Martin and the beeping machines. Her eyes were moist and frightened. "Is it bad?" she whispered.

"Please take a seat," the nurse repeated. "It's better if the doctor explains everything. And you'd better go now, young lady."

The latter was addressed to me, of course. I left. But I couldn't help looking over my shoulder. Mrs Winter sat on the plastic chair in her dripping wet coat. The only thing she'd taken off was a glove. She'd placed her hand on top of Martin's, and I could hear her whispering to him. It sounded like "Oh, my poor boy. My poor boy..."

Everyone I knew was scared of Martin to at least some extent. Even Oscar. So it was weird to hear someone call him "my poor boy". And even weirder coming from an old lady not much taller than me.

I had no idea that Martin lived with his grandmother. People from his own year might know, but I'd never heard anything about it. At school we know pretty much all there is to know about each other – whose parents are divorced, who lives where. But when everyone's scared of you, maybe they don't ask too many questions.

I'd almost returned to my bed in A&E when I heard someone call out.

"Mousie!"

"Mum..."

She, too, was dripping wet. Rain had flattened her hair and darkened the fabric of her white down jacket. Somewhere outside the hospital it was probably still daylight, almost spring, and it was raining. In here, the whole world seemed to consist of blue linoleum floors, dark blue walls, fluorescent tubes and a pervasive smell of detergent.

I snuggled up to her.

"I couldn't find you," she said. "They told me you were here, but you weren't."

"I'm here now."

"Yes. Are you OK, Mouse?"

"Pretty much," I said. "I just feel a bit weird. And I'd really like to go home now, please."

On our way home in the car, the rain pelted the roof and the windscreen wipers squeaked as they swished from side to side. Cat had curled up on my lap. It would take someone very brave to order him into a cat carrier, and Mum wasn't foolish enough to try.

"Are you hungry?" she said.

"Don't know really..." I still felt a bit odd. Was it possible to feel nauseous and absolutely ravenous at the same time?

"Fancy some pear tart?"

I smiled, mostly for her sake, and said: "Well, if you're offering pear tart, then..." I didn't want to make her any more worried than she already was.

We stopped outside the bakery and I stayed in the car while Mum went to get the tart.

"Were you serious?" I asked Cat. "When you said I accidentally took Martin along on my Journeying and then... dropped him."

Do I normally say things I don't mean?

No. He didn't. During all the time I'd known him, he'd always said exactly what he meant. Even though he couldn't say anything out loud, he never left me in any doubt.

"Does that mean it's my fault?" I asked. "Martin and... the hospital and... everything?"

Fault? Cat sounded as if he didn't know the meaning of the word. *What do you mean?*

"My mistake. My fault."

He arched his back and stretched so that his black tail brushed right past my nose. Then he let out a big, pink yawn.

What does that have to do with anything?

I didn't know, but it was hugely important to me. Martin lying there with tubes coming out of his arm and all the flashing machines and a granny who was soaked to the skin muttering "my poor boy" over and over again... all of that was bad enough. If Martin had fallen from a bike shed, hurt himself badly, and the whole thing was an accident, then that was bad enough. But if I was responsible for dropping him...

"Fsssttt..." Cat snorted in a very feline way. *Humans.*

"But what if?"

Either it has nothing to do with you, Cat said, leaving me with the feeling that it certainly had nothing to do with him. *Or...*

"Or what?"

Or you can do something about it.

"But... there's nothing I can do!"

Then it has nothing to do with you.

But it had.

Mum came half running down the pavement, tore open the door and shoved a white box into my hands.

"Take this," she said, "before it gets completely soaked." She got in, and slammed shut the door.

"Mum..."

"Yes, Mouse?"

"I'm not allowed back to school for the rest of the week."

"No, they told me. Never mind, we can have a nice time together at home." My mum was a freelance journalist and worked from home, except when she went out to talk to people and investigate the things she wrote about.

"Yes, but... I was thinking... would it be OK if instead I... went to see Aunt Isa?"

The smile disappeared. It would not be OK. She would hate it, I was well aware of that.

Then she pulled herself together and put the smile back on as though it was an itchy sweater she was determined to wear in order to please me.

"Of course, darling," she said. "Who knows, perhaps the badger has had her babies."

She was making a big effort. And the stinging and prickling inside me worsened because I could see how miserable she was underneath the itchy-sweater smile.

Humans. Why do you have to make everything so complicated? Cat clearly wasn't expecting an answer because he'd already curled up on my lap with his nose under his tail. Ten seconds later he was fast asleep.

CHAPTER EIGHT

Soul Tangle

Mum drove me all the way to Aunt Isa's the next day. It took hours, but she didn't want us to use the wildways.

"Not when you're poorly," she said, and I decided not to mention that several hours in our little Kia made me carsick and that that was definitely worse than the wildways. Though to be fair, the wildways *were* dangerous. They could kill you if you lost your way, but Cat never did.

Aunt Isa was out. Bumble, too, was gone, and the badger snarled at us from the dog basket – she still hadn't given birth.

"Isa will be back shortly," The Nothing said. "She is just giving Kahla a lesson somewhere in the woods. Would you like a cup of tea in the meantime? I can almost make it myself now, I just need someone to help me lift the kettle."

"No, thank you," said Mum without looking at The Nothing. "I'd better get back."

Then she gave me a hug, blew a raspberry on my neck and drove off.

"I don't think your mum likes me," The Nothing said sadly.

"Why not?"

"She didn't even want to look at me."

It was true. Mum had been busy looking in every other direction as if it hurt her eyes to look at the little girl's face in the midst of all the birdness.

"My mum doesn't like witchery and the wild-world," I said. "I think it scares her. Or rather she's scared that something might happen to me. And you are... very wildwitchy."

"Do you think so?"

"People can tell from looking at you that you were made by a wildwitch. Or... someone who was once a wildwitch."

The Nothing furrowed her feathery eyebrows.

"Is that bad?" she wanted to know.

"No, it's just... unusual."

"Unusual." She tasted the word. "So I'm... unusual."

"Yes. And that's good," I declared firmly, because otherwise she would have worried about that, too, and decided that it was another bad thing.

She smiled so that I could see almost all her

tiny, white teeth. They were a little sharper than human teeth, and I was reminded of the flock of shark-mouthed, flying sisters she was supposed to have become part of; that is, if she hadn't been a "failure".

"Please would you help me with the kettle?" she said.

And when Aunt Isa and Kahla came home a little later with a very muddy and happy Bumble at their heels, an excited Nothing flew to meet them.

"I made tea, I made tea, I made tea..." she chanted.

"How wonderful," Aunt Isa said. "Clara! How nice to see you."

"Mum drove me," I said.

Aunt Isa raised an eyebrow. "Did she now? That was very kind of her." It was more than kind, it was borderline heroic, and Aunt Isa knew it. "Has she left already?"

"She wanted to get home before it got dark."

"Of course, it's a long journey by car."

"Come drink your tea while it's hot," The Nothing said. "I made it myself! I took the tea caddy from the shelf, then I found the spoon, then I opened the caddy, then I took the strainer, then I measured out the tea with a spoon – a spoon for each cup and one for the pot – and then... Clara helped me with the boiling water."

"Thank you so much," Aunt Isa said. Kahla rolled her eyes, but fortunately The Nothing didn't notice. "I do love coming home to a nice cup of tea. But Clara – you look a bit under the weather. What's wrong?"

"I fell off the roof of the bike shed." I would prefer to tell her the rest once Kahla had gone home. I didn't know why. Possibly because I still didn't like revealing what a rubbish wildwitch I was. Kahla would never have dropped Martin. Kahla had that Journeying stuff totally nailed.

"Brrr, it's so cold," Kahla said, looking as if she wanted to hug the stove. "Isn't it ever spring here?"

The sun was shining. Aunt Isa's small garden was full of snowdrops and celandines, and the whitethorn down by the brook were in flower. The Nothing looked confused.

"I thought it *was* spring?" she said.

"And so it is," Aunt Isa said. "But it's probably still not warm enough for Kahla."

Kahla's dad, Master Millaconda, came to fetch her half an hour later. Kahla ran to meet him; not just because she was excited to see him, I thought, but also because she was dying to go home and be warm.

"Right," Aunt Isa said. "So what happened?" She could tell that there was more to the story than me getting a bit bruised and battered. I told her about the lasagne and the grass snake, and about Martin and the flying.

"The nurse said it takes a lot to break a shoulder blade," I said. "He thought Martin must have fallen from something a lot higher than a bike shed. And Martin smelled like a squirrel."

"And you could smell that even after you came back from your Journeying?"

"Yes."

"It wasn't just something Cat could smell?"

"No, I could smell it too."

"Let me take a look at you."

I was sitting right in front of her, she couldn't avoid seeing me, but she meant with her wildsense. She took my hands, closed her eyes and started humming a wildsong; it was a bit like being X-rayed all over again, only in a witchy sort of way.

Suddenly she let go of me, so abruptly that my hands flopped onto my lap with a soft bump. Her eyes flew open and if it hadn't been impossible – I mean, we're talking about Aunt Isa here – then I would have said that she almost looked... scared.

"There is something..." she said. "Something inside you, all tangled up with something else. I would call it a soul tangle. A large knot of life cords and... and..."

"And what?"

"Death. No, more than just natural death. *Deadness*. It's all wrong."

The Nothing looked frightened.

"Is Clara all wrong too?" she asked.

Aunt Isa didn't reply immediately.

"Clara is Clara," she said at length. "And we very much want that to continue. But we had better get Mrs Pommerans to take a look at you."

"Why?" I asked. Mrs Pommerans was nice, an older wildwitch who had backed me when I had to convince the Raven Mothers that I'd told them the truth about Chimera. But I had greater faith in Aunt Isa.

"She's better than me at this sort of thing," Aunt Isa said. "Are you tired? Would you like to rest or should we get going right away? You can ride Star if you like."

"Let's get it over and done with," I said darkly.

The Nothing looked disappointed.

"Does that mean you won't want any more tea?" she asked.

Mrs Pommerans lived in an apple orchard, not far from Aunt Isa's house – that is, when you went by the wildways. It took us only a few minutes.

The apple trees were already in blossom, and it felt warmer here than back at Aunt Isa's, or back home in Mercury Street for that matter. There were daffodils in the grass among the dark trunks of the apple trees, some of them had opened and were nodding their fine yellow heads in the gentle breeze.

"How come it's so warm here?" I wanted to know. "We haven't travelled that far, have we?"

"I have a hunch that Mrs Pommerans cheats a little," Aunt Isa said. "But don't tell anyone. The Raven Mothers disapprove strongly of anyone tinkering with the weather, and it can very easily go wrong." She raised her voice. "Hello? Agatha, are you in?"

Mrs Pommerans appeared behind a picket fence. She'd been planting spinach in her vegetable garden, we discovered. Her green trousers had muddy knees, and her floral print gardening gloves were black with potting compost.

"Oh, hello, Isa. And Clara. How nice to see you again, dear."

"How lovely and mild it is here," Aunt Isa exclaimed with a twinkle in her eyes. "You must be very lucky with the weather."

"Yes," Mrs Pommerans said innocently. "We're so sheltered from the winds..."

Aunt Isa grew serious again.

"Agatha, I hope you can help us. Clara has run into some... Journeying difficulties. And something's not right."

"I see." Mrs Pommerans studied me calmly, as she dusted soil off her knees. "Then we'd better take a look at her... but please first tie up Star, I seem to remember that she has an unfortunate taste for apple blossoms."

I slipped down from Star's warm back, and we tied her to the picket fence that surrounded the vegetable garden. It might have been all in my mind, but I'm sure she looked a little put out. I patted her neck.

"You'll get an extra helping of hay when we get home," I promised.

Mrs Pommerans's house was at the heart of the orchard, half-timbered and under a slightly too moss-grown thatched roof. The door was apple green, and so were the curtains and the carpets, as it turned out when we went inside.

"You sit yourself down there," Mrs Pommerans said, pointing to a high-backed chair upholstered with green velvet. "And let me have a look at you..."

She did exactly what Aunt Isa had done, except that her wildsong was slower and somehow milder. Her weather-worn hands were warm, I started yawning and was afraid that I might nod off if she went on for much longer. My whole body was humming and buzzing, but not in an unpleasant way, just... drowsily.

"Oh dear, what a mess," Mrs Pommerans said at length. "It's impossible to see which way's up in that dog's breakfast of a soul tangle."

Aunt Isa shook her head.

"No, I couldn't find a solution either. And there are more than just life cords, there are also... death threads."

Death threads... That didn't sound good at all.

Mrs Pommerans bent down, stuck her hand under the sofa and pulled out a basket. It was filled with balls of yarn and knitting needles. She held up an unfinished piece of knitting – it looked like it was going to be a jumper. The yarn was – no surprise there – apple green, but with yellow stripes.

"I believe Isa has told you about life cords," she said. "You know what they are?"

I nodded. All living things had a cord that connected them to the rest of the world. If it was cut, you died. Normally it was invisible, but you could feel it. And a skilled wildwitch could see it with her wildsense.

"There tends to be a pattern. An order in the way we're connected to the world and to each other," Mrs Pommerans said, adjusting her spectacles slightly.

"Take this piece of knitting. It looks dense and fine, and you may think it's made up of several pieces of string, but in fact it's all one and the same." She held up the yarn between the knitting and the ball. "But when I look at you now, there's something else. You look more like this..."

At the bottom of the basket there was a tangled mess of yarn in many different colours: white, yellow, dark green, apple green, pink.

"You try untangling that," she said, handing me the basket. "It's good practice. Meanwhile I'll do some thinking."

She sat down in a green rocking chair by the window from where she could see the apple trees. She started rocking back and forth while she hummed to herself and began knitting almost as if we weren't there.

I frowned and looked at Aunt Isa. I'd expected more.

"Get on with it," she said softly, pointing to the tangled yarn. "She has her reasons..."

I picked up the end of the dark-green yarn and tried following it through the "dog's breakfast". If that was how I looked on the inside, no wonder I had a headache...

It was hard. Hard to concentrate as I sat here, and I grew increasingly sleepy. And it was fiddly to disentangle the yarn without tightening the knots even more. At the same time, my hands seemed to grow cold and numb. My head flopped forwards and I sat up with a jerk. Yawned. Tried again. Tried the pale-green yarn. Perhaps that would be easier...

Beep. Beep. Beep.

There was a faint hum around me. I was cold, not just my hands, but all over, even though the room was warm. My eyelids were incredibly heavy and I could no longer tell the threads of yarn apart.

"We haven't had any conscious response from him yet, Mrs Winter," someone said. "And to be honest – there are areas of his brain where we can detect no normal function. I think we need to prepare ourselves for the possibility that there may be damage, but it's hard to assess the extent as long as he remains in a coma."

The skeleton of the little sparrow was lying among the stripped, dead leaves. The dried-out hide of the grass snake was falling apart, scale by scale. On the forest floor, in the middle of the death zone, the dust stirred, it moved and began to form a pattern.

Beep. Beep. Beep.

My wings grew tired. My talons could barely hold onto the branch. My head slumped heavily onto my chest.

I was hungry. I was hunger itself. Not just hungry after a lean winter, it was much, much more than that. I was so starved that I could swallow up the whole world. Come... Come here, little bird, little grass snake. Come here, little squirrel.

Come to me. Mummy is hungry...

"Clara." It was Mrs Pommerans. Her face was very close to mine, her hands grabbing my shoulders. "Clara, that's enough now."

"I'm hungry..." I whimpered, and didn't quite recognize my own voice. "I'm starving."

"I'll give you some food in a moment," Mrs Pommerans said. "But right now... I think you'd better let go of the yarn."

I looked down. The tangled yarn hadn't grown any less tangled, quite the opposite. But something else had happened. The yarn had turned cobweb grey, and my icy fingers were covered in grey dust.

I made a strangled little sound and tried to toss aside the yarn, but it stuck to my crooked, cold, grey fingers, and Aunt Isa had to help free me.

"Here," Mrs Pommerans said. "Eat this..."

I was barely aware of what I was stuffing into my mouth. Only slowly did I begin to taste apple, sweetness, a crisp crust – it was apple pie, and eventually it started to sate some of the terrible, hungry emptiness inside me.

"What's happening?" I said. "What is happening to me?"

Mrs Pommerans examined the tangled, dusty grey yarn carefully.

"A sparrow," she said. "A grass snake. A boy. A hawk. A squirrel. And... something else. Something that's dead, but still hungry." She looked up. "The sparrow and the grass snake are dead. The hawk, the squirrel and the boy are alive. We can't just cut you loose, or they'll die too."

"Then what?" I pressed her. "How do we make it... stop?"

"I need more time to think about that..." Mrs Pommerans said.

They weren't the words I wanted to hear. I wanted her to say: "Here's a cup of magic herbal tea. Drink it and everything will be all right," or words to that effect. But she didn't. She just looked as if we had handed her a mess she had no idea how to clean up.

CHAPTER NINE

New-Born Life

It had been some time since I last slept in Aunt Isa's attic room, now "my" room, at least when I was visiting. It was snug and cosy with a round window in the end wall, a sloping ceiling and a rag rug in front of the bed. In my absence, a couple of cardboard boxes had found their way into a corner, but that didn't really matter; pretty much all of Aunt Isa's house looked like that.

"Does anything live in those?" I asked and pointed.

Aunt Isa smiled. "No," she said, "they are just bits and bobs for my painting and a little extra birdseed. How's your head?"

"OK." And it was, despite the trip to Mrs Pommerans's house and back. "But... I'm still a bit hungry..."

"Still? You must have hit a growth spurt. How about a sandwich?"

"Yes, please."

One sandwich turned into three and I had to clean my teeth again, and when I came back upstairs, Bumble had made himself comfortable on my bed.

"Move it!" I said.

And he did – just enough so that I could crawl under the duvet next to him. I could have made him get down on the floor, but it was nice and reassuring to fall asleep with a warm, heavy dog as my radiator.

I woke because my stomach was screaming with hunger. Or no – not my stomach. It still felt bloated after all those sandwiches. However, *something* inside me cried out for food, and although I tried to ignore it and go back to sleep, it didn't work.

Moonlight was streaming through the round window, and next to me Bumble was snoring his gigantic, rumbling dog snore. I eased my left arm free of the duvet to check my watch. It was three o'clock in the morning. There was absolutely no good reason for me to be wanting to eat a horse.

"Go back to sleep," I whispered to myself. "Forget about food."

Food. Foodfoodfoodfoodfood. Now!

I gave in. With bare legs and in stockinged feet the attic room was quite chilly, as were the stairs, but the kitchen downstairs was warmer. I had already taken the bread from the bread bin when I became aware of another scent. The fresh, red, wet smell of blood and new-born baby animals.

I put down the bread and sniffed the air again. There could be no doubt.

In the living room the badger mum was half-lying, half-sitting in the basket, licking five tiny, glistening, dark bundles. My belly rumbled. New life. Fresh, new-born life... Not tired and half-starved after winter, but covered in birth fat, juicy and full of –

No. What?? I...

The badger raised her head and sniffed the air. Then she twisted violently and scrambled to her feet, although her hip was not yet fully healed. She growled deep in her throat and snarled so the moonlight reflected blue and white in her teeth.

"Easy now," I whispered, as softly as I could. "I would never hurt your babies..."

Life. Brand new life...

My earlier appetite was nothing compared to the wave of black hunger welling up inside me now. I wanted those cubs. I wanted to swallow them, crunch them, devour them. I wanted to drink their blood, drain their juices and their life, I wanted to suck the marrow out of their tender bones, I wanted—

No, I did not.

I most definitely did not want that sort of hunger.

It was the single most disgusting thing I had ever felt, and it was *inside* me. I'd taken three steps towards the cubs without even meaning to, the mother was still weak after the birth and posed no real threat, I could easily have...

No. Nonono.

"Go away!" I screamed. "Leave me! **Goaway, goaway, goaway...**"

Something split. With a wet snap something left me, forcing its way out. It felt as if my ribs snapped and my skin was peeled back. I think I screamed, but I'm not sure. I thought I saw a shadow, a dark splodge, an outline in the moonlight, but it wasn't any shape that I recognized, just a tangled, living darkness that lunged towards the badger and its cubs in a sudden, unstoppable leap.

"No! *Go away!*"

I didn't make it stop, but Cat did.

Suddenly he was there, the size of a panther, right in the middle of the living room, in front of the badger. He let out the most piercing, hateful cat scream I'd ever heard, and his claws grew as long

as knives. He and the darkness merged and turned into a hissing, fighting, screaming bundle of cat fur, claws and weird shadows. The badger mum collapsed clumsily and I just stood there with my hand pressed against my chest to keep my heart from popping out.

And all of a sudden it was over.

Cat fell bonelessly to the floor. He was no longer a panther. Just a limp, skinny cat, more grey than black, whose skin and fur hung so loosely over his frame that it looked as if he had been stripped of every last scrap of muscle and fat.

"Cat!"

I threw myself on my knees beside him, but was suddenly afraid to touch him.

"What's going on...?"

Aunt Isa appeared in the doorway in her dressing gown and with bare feet. She looked from the badger to Cat and then at me. There was an expression of disbelief on her face that I later would find very, very hard to forget.

"Clara," she said slowly. "What have you done?"

CHAPTER TEN

Darkest Night

"**I**s he dead?"

I hardly dared ask, didn't dare touch him, didn't dare move.

"No," Aunt Isa said. "Not quite. But... there's not much left." Carefully, she picked up Cat's limp body and held him close. He didn't take up much room in her arms.

"Boil the kettle and fill a couple of hot water bottles," she said. "He's as cold as ice..."

I jumped up, relieved there was something I could do, so I wouldn't have to sit still and think. Think and remember... No.

The Nothing came flapping across the floor from the bedroom, even clumsier than usual because she was still sleepy and confused.

"What happened?" she asked. "Who was screaming?"

"Cat," I said. "He... no, I don't want to talk about

it right now. Please would you help me find some hot water bottles?"

The Nothing blinked. "I can find them for you," she said. "But I won't be able to lift them."

Aunt Isa had fetched a pillow and half wrapped it around Cat while still holding him tight so that she could share the heat from her body with him.

"Let's see if we can get some sugar water inside him," she said, and started humming a wildsong, wordless and deep.

The badger had returned to the basket and curled up protectively around her young, but she seemed calmer now, and she was no longer looking at me.

I went to the kitchen and filled up the big kettle. What had happened to me? How on earth could I... how on earth could anyone even think of eating... no, the thought was revolting. *Inside* me. Yeeeeeugh. And Cat...

My brain whirled and my thoughts started churning of their own accord, even though I tried to stop them. Cat. Limp and grey, no bigger than an ordinary house cat. What had happened? Was it really me – or something inside me? What had I done to him?

"Please don't die," I whispered, although I didn't think he could hear me. "Please don't..." Bumble nudged me with his nose, wanting to be patted, or perhaps he was just looking for comfort. I put my hand on his big, warm head and started to cry.

"I don't want to be evil..." I whispered into his soft fur.

"Evil?" said The Nothing, and then she sneezed. "What does that mean? Is it bad?"

"Yes," I said. "It's... it's really bad."

"Then I don't think you are," she declared. "The hot water bottles are in the green wooden box on the shelf under the gardening books."

Aunt Isa told me to fetch an old dog basket from the attic – too small for Bumble, but the right size for Cat when lined with a warm blanket, hot water bottles and one of my jumpers. Aunt Isa placed the basket next to the wood-burning stove so he'd be warm, but when she tried to get some sugar water into him with a straw, it just trickled out of the corner of his mouth and down across the fur on his neck.

"It was me who found the hot-water bottles," The Nothing said. "I knew where they were, only I couldn't lift them myself!"

"Good girl," Aunt Isa said patiently. "I'm glad that someone in this house knows where everything is." She sang some more wildsong for Cat, and I thought I could finally see his breathing grow deeper and steadier.

Then she turned to me.

"What happened?" she said, and her gaze was sharper than most surgical instruments. There was no point in lying.

"I... I was so hungry. I..." I stared desperately at the floor. "Aunt Isa, there's something wrong with me. I felt like... I wanted to... If Cat hadn't..."

"Was it the cubs?" Aunt Isa asked quietly. "The newborns?"

I raised my head in amazement. How could she know?

"How did you know?" I whispered.

"Somewhere in that... tangle... something wants to live. Something that's dead, or almost dead. Something that doesn't just kill to eat like a normal predator, but takes everything – body, soul, life force, everything. Life. More than anything it craves life. And nothing is more alive than that which has only just been born."

"You said... you said I'd done something."

"No, I don't believe I did."

"Yes. You said... you asked me what I'd done. Is it me, Aunt Isa? Is it my fault? Am I... am I becoming evil?"

"Oh, my darling girl." Aunt Isa pulled me close and gave me a long, warm hug, something she very rarely did. "It's not that simple. Evil isn't a single big thing, something you just are or become. It's a hundred little things, a hundred selfish, hurtful thoughts, a hundred wicked acts... It's not an either-or. "

"I don't understand..."

"We all have evil in us – and good as well. And plenty in-between. You don't suddenly wake up one morning having turned evil overnight."

"But what I felt... what I wanted to do. Aunt Isa, that was evil!"

"That hunger wasn't yours. Or rather, it wasn't just yours. Think about the yarn. Only some of those threads come from you. But if you're not strong enough, the hunger can use you." She placed her hands on my shoulders and looked into my eyes. "You can't afford to be scared or lazy or selfish or weak."

"Is that what I am?"

"That's not what I said. On the contrary, I think you can become a fine and strong human being, and a very good wildwitch. If you want to. And right now... right now we all need you to do that. Otherwise..."

"Otherwise what?"

"Otherwise you'll lose. And then that dead, hungry creature can get at the rest of us through you."

I wasn't hungry now. In fact, I couldn't imagine ever being hungry again. But if Aunt Isa was right, all I'd done was buy time before the hunger returned. Or rather – Cat had won that time for me. I slumped to my knees by the basket, and cautiously rested my hand on Cat's head. He was still far too cold, not the warm living creature he usually was.

"You're saying it's my fault," I whispered. "Because I wasn't strong enough."

"Fault," Aunt Isa heaved a sigh. "It doesn't matter whose fault it is, Clara! It's about stopping it. Finding that dead thing, whatever it is. Making it release you, Cat, the boy from your school, the squirrel and the hawk, release everything it has stolen or is trying to steal."

"But how can I?" I practically shouted. "Not even Mrs Pommerans knows how. She said she would think about it, but we haven't heard a word from her. So she doesn't know either. Or she just doesn't care..."

"Clara! Stop it. It's not her fault either."

I rubbed my face with one hand. My skin felt alien and dead under my fingers, as if it belonged to someone else.

"No," I muttered. But I couldn't help thinking that it would be so much easier if it were.

CHAPTER ELEVEN

The Revenant

I sat beside the basket all night. Aunt Isa went to bed, but set the egg timer to go off every hour so that she could sing to Cat again, looking more and more tired each time she did so.

Just as the morning sun was starting to paint the black branches green and brown, I heard cooing and scrambling by the kitchen window. I stood up stiffly. A fat pigeon was sitting outside, tapping the glass with its beak. I let it in. It had a small note tied around one leg with green yarn.

I wasn't used to carrier pigeons, so it took me several minutes to untie the yarn. The pigeon tucked its beak into its chest feathers in a mildly irritated fashion, but it put up with my butterfingers.

"Coooo, cooo," it said.

"All right, all right, I'm doing it as fast as I can."

The note was from Mrs Pommerans, obviously. There was a stamp on the outside, an apple with an elaborate P inside it. I unfolded the thin piece of paper in haste.

Find out who the hungry one is, it said in the same loopy handwriting as the P.

"Is that it?" I said, looking accusingly at the pigeon. "She spent the whole night thinking, and this is all she has to show for it?"

"You don't write long messages for carrier pigeons," said Aunt Isa behind me. I jumped because I hadn't heard her come in.

"She could at least have written a bit about how," I protested. "There would have been room for that."

"As soon as Kahla arrives, she can take you there. Then you can ask her yourself."

It was obvious why Aunt Isa couldn't take me. She had to stay with Cat. Even a half-baked, rubbish wildwitch like me could see that her wildsong was the only thing keeping him alive.

Kahla and her dad arrived a little later, just after Aunt Isa had finished singing for Cat one more time.

"Run and ask Master Millaconda if he would be kind enough to come inside," Aunt Isa said.

Normally he would just walk Kahla through the wildways fog and say goodbye to her by the gate, a bit like when Mum drove me to school and dropped me off. I had a hunch Aunt Isa wanted to know if he could help Cat.

When I caught up with them, Master Millaconda was about to leave. As usual Kahla was protected by a colourful cocoon of caps, coats and gloves, and Master Millaconda, too, was warmly dressed in a brown camel coat with a brown-and-white checked scarf and a brown felt hat that looked a bit like the ones worn by old-fashioned detectives. His dark-brown shoes were shiny and smelled of shoe polish. He tipped his hat politely when he saw me.

"Clara. How are you doing?"

"Not so good," I said, which was something of an understatement. "In fact Aunt Isa wanted to know if you have time to come in."

"Of course," he replied.

It turned out it wasn't just Cat that Aunt Isa wanted Master Millaconda to take a look at. It was me, too. She ushered him over to the badger basket and spoke to him in a low voice, but it didn't take a genius to work out what she was saying. My cheeks burned with shame.

"What's wrong with him?" asked Kahla, who was squatting on her haunches next to Cat. "It's almost as if he is not really here anymore..."

"Don't say that!"

"Sorry. I didn't mean to..."

"No. But just don't."

Kahla looked up at me with her clear, dark eyes.

"I haven't found a wildfriend yet," she said. "But I can imagine how you feel."

I wasn't so sure; after all, she didn't know that Cat was lying there, grey and shrunken and practically lifeless, because of me.

"Clara. Could we step outside for a moment?" Master Millaconda said.

I looked at Aunt Isa. She nodded. And so there really was nothing else but to do it.

"I'm sorry it's so cold out here," Kahla's dad said. "But I need the sun." Bumble had followed us and went to pee up against the apple trees and the fruit bushes in the orchard. From the stable Star whinnied, thinking I was bringing her hay.

"It won't hurt," Master Millaconda said, which only made me tense up even more.

He placed a gloved hand on each of my shoulders and started chanting something that sounded completely different from Aunt Isa's wildsong, yet somehow was still the same. I guess he carried on for about ten minutes. Bumble padded over to us and sniffed Master Millaconda's leg, but I don't think he even noticed.

When he stopped, he watched me for a few more moments.

"Are you hungry now?" he asked.

"No."

"Remarkable."

"Why?"

"Your aunt told me about the badger cubs."

I'd guessed as much, but even so I went red again.

"I don't know what came over me..." I said.

"I think that Isa is right when she says you might have an uninvited guest. Possibly a revenant."

"A what?"

"A revenant. Someone who is trying to return to life."

"A ghost?"

"Not quite. What you call a ghost is usually a dead person whose spirit still walks the earth."

"Isn't that the same thing?"

"No. Revenants aren't content with being spirits or ghosts. They want to live again, body and all."

Mrs Pommerans had said there was something dead in my soul tangle. Something dead but hungry at the same time. I shuddered.

"Is that even possible?"

"Yes, unfortunately. If the hungry one takes enough lives."

"So was the hungry one... trying... to take me? Take my life?"

"It sounds more like it was trying to take life *through* you. And when you expelled it with your simple, but strangely effective invocation..."

"Go away?"

"Yes. When you did that, Cat attacked and pulled it away."

"Where to?"

"Back into the soul tangle, as far as I can tell. Right now he's keeping the hungry one in check, and he won't let it get to you. You have a remarkable wildfriend."

"And that's why he is... the way he is?" Limp and lifeless. It was like someone had taken an ice pick to my gut and my conscience at the same time.

"I think so. He and the hungry one are keeping each other in a stand-off, that's why you're not hungry any more, but the struggle is so consuming that he barely has enough strength left to stay alive. And..."

"What?"

"I'm sorry to have to tell you this: he can't carry on."

The tears stung my tired eyes.

"What can I do?" I said. "What can I do to save him?"

"Kahla and I will take you to Mrs Pommerans now. You'll have to find your own way back to Isa because I have to go on from there."

"Where?" I asked, though it probably wasn't terribly polite. After all, it might be none of my business.

Or perhaps it was. At least he answered me.

"I need to speak to the Raven Mothers," he said.

"About me?"

"About you, among other things," he said.

CHAPTER TWELVE

Vademecum

Mrs Pommerans looked up as Kahla and I approached. She was sitting in the sunshine in front of her house with a basket on her lap, busy sorting seeds into home-made envelopes on which she had written in her neat, old-fashioned handwriting: *spinach* and *marigold* and so on.

"You look very serious," she said.

"My dad thinks Clara has been visited by a revenant," Kahla said.

Mrs Pommerans pursed her lips.

"A revenant," she then said, and it wasn't a question. "Now, that is... serious."

Anger rose inside me, hot and sudden. I wasn't entirely sure where it came from, but it had something to do with all that scrutiny, all their gloomy assumptions and their anxious faces. I was fed up with being probed and studied. And I was even more fed up that some kind of spectre seemed to be making its comeback through me. Who exactly had decided that I would be the ball in the big pinball game of life, so that everyone, living or dead, could just flip me around whenever they felt like it?

"Tell me what to do," I said. "Cat is dying, and I... I can't stand it any longer. There has to be something I can do!"

Mrs Pommerans gave me yet another one of those scrutinizing adult looks I'd had more than enough of.

"Finally," she said with a faint smile. "I do believe you're ready."

"Ready?" I growled. "Ready for what?"

"Clara, sweetheart, you can't help the way you've been brought up. You've resisted all along, and no wonder. But it's hard to become a good wildwitch when something inside you is constantly pulling the other way."

"Just tell me how I can save Cat," I demanded.

"The answer hasn't changed: find out who the hungry one is."

"But *how*?"

"Right now you just want someone to lash out at, and I can understand that. But you need to look inside yourself for some of the answers. Not all enemies can be vanquished from the outside."

I felt like shaking her small, gentle figure until her head bobbed. I didn't because a small, tired, doubting voice in my head was asking if the angry person really was me, or if the rage was seeping out of the soul tangle like the hunger had earlier.

I think Mrs Pommerans could see both the rage and the doubt.

"Come inside with me," she said. "I have something for you."

It turned out to be a small, round silver box with a crescent moon on the lid.

"Be careful when you open it," she said.

I did as I was told. The box contained a fine, pale-green powder whose scent was mild and heavy at the same time.

"What is it?" I asked.

"Vademecum powder. Vademecum is Latin, but it just means 'come with me'. It'll give you vivid and fruitful dreams."

"Why is it called that?"

"I think it was originally intended as a joke. A very wildwitch sort of joke... I suppose the idea is that the powder takes you into dreams, sometimes whether you want to or not. Other people just call it dream dust."

I eyed the small, round tin suspiciously.

"Is it a kind of sleeping potion?"

"No. It won't make you sleepy. It affects your dreams, not your sleep. Some people use it to make Journeying easier, sharper and more insightful."

"Is that why you're giving it to me?"

She gave me a mild, but piercing look.

"You're not really going Journeying," she said. "You are not going outwards, but inwards into the soul tangle. You need to find the thread that belongs to the hungry one and follow it. That is, if you dare."

I would be lying if I tried to pretend I wasn't scared half to death. I had no urge whatsoever to go looking for that disgusting, insatiable black creature.

"Why?" I said. "I thought we were trying to make it go away, not seek it out."

"You can't conquer it until you've found it," Mrs Pommerans said patiently. "And you won't find it until you know what it is."

Fair point.

"Right," I said. "So how do I use this stuff?"

"Dip your fingertip in it and brush it between your eyes, like this." She touched my forehead with a warm forefinger, and trailed it gently down past my eyebrows until she reached the top of my nose. "But remember – only a tiny amount."

My finger was shaking. As was the rest of my hand. But I took a little of the green powder and did as I was told.

Almost instantly, the world went away.

CHAPTER THIRTEEN

The Grotto

"Kimmie?"

I yawned and scratched myself above the eye. Why was I so sleepy?

"Kimmie, you've had enough time to rest! Come on!"

The impatient voice was accompanied by a shove from a sharp elbow.

"All right, all right..."

Slowly I rose to my feet and brushed moss and leaves off my skirt. Slanted, shimmering beams of sunlight fell between the tree trunks and it was baking hot. Insects buzzed around us, and we still had lots of lovely long time left before it got dark and we'd have to be back at school.

Pavola marched along the path in front of me. As always, her grey school uniform was as immaculate as her glossy, dark hair. It was only ever me who ended up with moss stains on my knees and twigs in my hair. I wished I were like Pavola: clever, attractive, perfect. But I wasn't. I had no idea why she even bothered being friends with me.

Pine branches rustled above my head and a nuthatch darted down a tree trunk with the speed of a squirrel. It stopped almost right by my hand and turned its neck to look at me.

I stood completely still. The nuthatch made a half turn around itself and watched me, calm and unruffled. I felt a pang of longing in my chest, but I suppressed it hard. Never again. I'd once loved a bird too much, and it had proved to be once too often.

"Kimmie, hurry up, or we'll be late..."

"I'm coming, I'm coming..."

Wait. Stop. Suddenly I was in two minds. What was going on? Who was I, and who was Pavola? My name wasn't Kimmie. My name was...

Then my doubts evaporated. Of course my name was Kimmie. What else would it be? And Pavola was my best friend at Oakhurst Academy. She had been ever since my arrival two years ago when I was new and stupid and didn't know anyone or where to sit in the dining hall. It was then that Pavola had smiled at me, made the others shift up on the bench and said: "You can sit here."

Now she was walking in front of me along the path, her dark ponytail bobbing up and down with each eager footstep.

"Is it far?" I asked.

"Quite far. That's why you need to get a move on."

"Can't we... cheat?"

Pavola stopped and turned around.

"Cheat? You mean... use the wildways?"

"Yes." My legs were starting to tire again and my body felt strangely drowsy and floppy, as if I were coming down with some bug. It was probably just the heat, but I had no wish to trek through the pine forest for hours just to see Pavola's "secret".

"Sniff can always tell, you know that."

Sniff was the headmistress's wildfriend, an old dachshund with a unique ability to detect even the faintest hint of wildways fog, no matter how careful we were. The students at Oakhurst Academy were allowed to move freely about the school grounds, but the wildways were strictly out of bounds unless you had special permission. Which we didn't.

"That dog is a pest," I said. "I wish it would choke to death on one of its stupid bones."

"Kimmie, don't say things like that. I know you don't mean it, but... just don't."

She was wrong. I did mean it. But I couldn't explain that to Pavola, who was not only pretty and perfect, but also sweet-natured and good to practically every kind of animal. She was one of those people who would rather flap aside a fly than squash it.

The walk ended up taking us all morning and a good part of the afternoon. It turned out we had to go all the way to the coast and, once we got there, Pavola insisted that we crawl through a dark, foul-smelling crack between two rocks.

"Pavola, it stinks."

"It's just seaweed. Come on, we're nearly there."

And then I had to creep and crawl and climb after her for the best part of another hour.

Her secret turned out to be a cave. In one way I could understand why Pavola was so proud of it. Had I been a bit younger, I too would probably have thought it was exciting and brilliant to know about a secret cave, and there was something almost magical about the light that fell through the cracks in its roof. But seriously – we'd already wasted half a precious day off getting here, and it would take us just as long to walk back.

"Great, Pavola. Can we go home now?"

Pavola looked disappointed and I felt a pang of guilt, but I said nothing.

"There's more," she said. "It's not just the cave..."

"Then what is it?"

"Here," she said as she started sweeping aside the sand on the cave floor. "Help me."

I heaved a sigh. Once Pavola had made up her mind, there was no stopping her. I knelt down and started brushing away the sand.

There was something underneath the sand. I could feel it with my wildsense almost the moment we started uncovering it. I got more excited and I stopped worrying about getting dirty or splitting two of my nails, which had just grown suitably long – that was another thing I argued with the headmistress about. "Talons like that belong on a bird of prey, Kimmie, not on human beings," she would invariably say and force me to cut them so that I would have to start all over again.

The floor under the sand in the grotto was flat. Completely flat and glassy, except for...

"That's the Wheel," I whispered. The Sun Wheel, the Cross Wheel, the Wheel of Life... it had many names, but to a wildwitch it had only one meaning: Everything. All of it. The whole world, the universe, everything. "What's it doing here?"

"I don't know," Pavola said. "It's always been here, or at least it has for as long as anyone in my family can remember. But... we're not supposed to show it to anyone."

"Why not?" I trailed my forefinger around the circumference of the wheel. It was big – one of the biggest I'd ever seen, maybe seven or eight metres across, with four spokes and a hub in the centre. "It's not the only Wheel in the world..."

"No, but... this one is special."

"Why?"

Pavola hesitated. "I don't know everything yet. They say I'm not old enough. When I turn fifteen, then... but that's ages away. All I know is that it's absolutely ancient and massively... massively important. And secret."

I already knew more than that. I could feel it. There was something in this cave, a power, a force, something just waiting to be unleashed. And I knew what it would take...

Quickly and without hesitation I swiped one of my unbroken nails across the palm of my left hand. I scratched myself as hard and as deeply as I could, and the blood started flowing immediately, not much, but enough.

"What are you doing?" Pavola cried out in alarm. "Don't. It's dangerous..."

I wasn't listening. I clenched and unclenched my hand a couple of times to force out even more blood and I let it drip onto the centre of the wheel, the hub, the heart of it all.

Nothing happened. At least, not straight away.

Pavola had thrown herself onto her knees and was wiping away the blood as fast as she could. For once her neat school uniform wasn't spotless – she had red smears of my blood on her sleeve.

"Kimmie!" she said. "I should never have brought you here."

"Why not?" I said. "Nothing happened."

And I suddenly knew why. My blood wasn't the right kind of blood. It would take a very special kind of blood to make this wheel spin. Something stirred inside me. A hunger. Not an ordinary hunger for food, or not just that. A hunger for life, for blood, for power. I bowed my head and sucked the blood from my torn palm. It helped a little, but I knew that it would take much more.

"Please don't tell anyone," Pavola said, looking at me nervously. "You won't, will you, Kimmie? You won't tell anyone, will you?"

"No," I said. "I won't."

I knew at that moment that Pavola and I were no longer friends. She was always so sweet and loyal... so it would take time before she worked it out and knew it too. But I could feel it loud and clear. Something had come between us, something violent, cold and dark, something which meant that I was now a thousand years old and she was still only fourteen. I wasn't going to reveal the secret of her cave. I had no interest in others knowing that it was there, and what it contained. It was enough that I knew.

"Kimmie?"

"What is it?"

"Are you... your hand. Does it hurt?"

"No."

I licked more blood from the scratch, but it had already started to close up again. Pavola looked at me.

"I should never have brought you here," she said again. And she was probably right.

CHAPTER FOURTEEN

Oakhurst Academy

I could hear cooing around me. I was lying on my
back on one of Mrs Pommerans's old quilts, and
four or five wood pigeons were mincing around
me, pecking at the grass and the twigs, completely
indifferent to the girl lying in their midst.

Slowly I sat up.

I wasn't Kimmie. It had all been a dream.

Kahla was sitting on the garden bench with
Mrs Pommerans, but as soon as I stirred, she leapt
up and a couple of offended pigeons flapped their
wings.

"So?" she said. "What happened?"

"Nothing." I touched my hair tentatively.
Smooth, mousey. Clara hair. Same as always. "Not
really..."

"What do you mean? It didn't work?"

"I just had a dream about two girls. Not... not
dead ones. Not revenants." The word felt strange and

alien in my mouth. "It was just a dream about some girls who discovered the cave below Westmark. You know, where Shanaia's family is from..." I looked to Mrs Pommerans. Of course she knew Shanaia, both of them had helped me against Chimera last autumn, but I wasn't sure if she'd ever visited Shanaia's childhood home.

"I've heard about it," was all she said. "What happened in your dream?"

I told them about Kimmie and Pavola. Mrs Pommerans listened attentively.

"It must be important," she said. "More important than you think." She had tipped seeds from the basket onto a plate and was removing some that didn't seem to belong. Every time she threw a seed on the ground, the wood pigeons would start to flap and argue over it, as if it were a chunk of bread.

"Silly birds," she chided them. "As if there isn't enough food around already..." Then she seemed to stop her train of thought. "Please tell me again," she said.

"All of it?" I said, somewhat overwhelmed.

"No. Just what happened in the cave."

"But... nothing really happened. The girls brushed the sand away and looked at the wheel. Kimmie tried dripping some of her blood onto it, but it didn't work. It wasn't the right blood."

"Was that everything?"

I struggled to explain the part about Kimmie suddenly knowing for sure that she and Pavola were no longer friends. I didn't understand why, but Kimmie had believed it was hugely, terribly important.

"She... Kimmie, I mean, she said... or rather, she didn't say anything, it was more what she was thinking. That they had grown apart, or something like that. That she was too old to be friends with Pavola. That something else was more important now."

Mrs Pommerans watched me through narrowed eyes.

"Yes. The question is what. Kahla?"

"Yes?"

"Do you know how to get to Oakhurst Academy?"

"Along the wildways?"

"Yes."

"Easily. I've been there three times with my dad," Kahla said. "He thought about sending me there when... when my mum..." Her smile faded, and she clearly had to steel herself to carry on. "... I mean, when she could no longer be responsible for my training. But I decided that I would rather study with Isa."

I'd never found out what really happened to Kahla's mother. All I knew was that she didn't live with Kahla and Master Millaconda anymore – Kahla had never said a word about why or where she had gone. Now was probably not a good time to ask.

"Kimmie and Pavola are quite unusual names," Mrs Pommerans said. "I think you should visit Oakhurst Academy and ask if anyone there knows them."

"Alone?" I said.

"No," Mrs Pommerans said. "With Kahla."

That wasn't what I meant, and she knew it. But after going on about how I wanted to do something, I didn't have the nerve to add that I would like a grown-up to come with me.

"Do you really think it will help save Cat?" I asked instead.

"All I know is that it'll be hard to save him if you don't go," Mrs Pommerans replied.

Oakhurst Academy looked more like a fortress than a school, or at least I thought so. But then again, I'd never seen a wildwitch boarding school before. It wasn't covered with turrets or surrounded by a moat, but it was built on a peninsula in a lake and there were embankments that a long time ago must have been part of a castle's fortifications. Now they looked peaceful and green, dotted with young

106

and old oak trees, and dark-grey sheep grazing on the slopes.

"It's seriously impressive," I said. "Why didn't you want to come here?"

Kahla hesitated.

"I don't think I'm that good at fitting in," she said. "And I think it's easier to be a student here if you are." She shrugged her shoulders, so that both her stripy scarves rose and sank. "Besides, it's quite expensive. I think my dad was relieved that I chose to study with Isa."

The bit about the money reminded me of something.

"Wasn't Oakhurst Academy the school Shanaia didn't want to be at?" I asked. "I mean, when her aunt Abigael died, and Chimera convinced everyone that Abigael had sold Westmark to her so that Shanaia could come here?"

"Yes, that's right. It's a really good school, but... I can understand why Shanaia didn't... fit in."

"And they kept all the money even though Shanaia ran away after only three weeks," I said. Suddenly the peaceful embankments and ivy-covered walls looked more hostile. "That's quite sneaky, don't you think?"

There was a fence and a gate, but the gate was open so we walked right into the courtyard that sat between the three wings of the school.

We'd arrived in the middle of a riding lesson, but it was unlike any riding lessons I'd ever known. Instead of seven or eight lazy ponies and horses, there were two elks, a heifer, a water buffalo, a wild donkey and a stag that trotted around with riders on their backs, though I saw no signs of saddles or bridles.

"Across the long diagonal, please," commanded the riding instructor, a grey-haired woman in a green jacket and skirt, and dusty, high-heeled shoes. "Nadya, do get him to trot with a *little* more energy!" This seemed to be directed at the girl on the water buffalo, because she straightened up and kicked the buffalo with her heels. The buffalo scowled, shook its head, and stopped abruptly so the wild donkey behind it nearly bumped into its broad, dark backside.

"No, no, no, Nadya. Don't use your legs! Use your mind, for God's sake. If you don't ask him nicely, of course he's going to get upset!" Then she spotted us. "Hello, girls. How can I help you?"

"We have a message for the headmistress," Kahla said.

"I see," the riding instructor said. "Nadya, for heaven's sake. Get him going again! Well, in that case, you may approach."

"Eh... are you the..."

"... the headmistress? Indeed I am. Edmina Stern. And wait... you're Millaconda's daughter, I believe? But you I don't recognize." She pointed a sharp finger at me.

"Clara Ash," I said as politely as I could. "Aunt Isa is my... well, my aunt."

"Oh yes, of course she is. Girls, walk the animals for five minutes, then return them to pasture. That's enough riding for today. And then it's straight to Egg-layer Psychology and Care of the Young, do I make myself clear? No hanging about the boys' wing!"

"Egg-layer Psychology?" I whispered to Kahla. "What on earth is that?"

Apparently I didn't whisper it quietly enough because Mrs Stern raised an eyebrow and replied: "Why, child. Hasn't Isa taught you anything? There's a world of difference between the personality of a mammal, where suckling creates a bond between the offspring and its mother, and the psychology of, for example, snakes and lizards that are hatched and never see their parents. Quite frankly, that sort of thing should be elementary knowledge for all wildwitches!"

"I'm not... erm, that's to say... I haven't been a wildwitch very long," I stammered. "Don't blame Aunt Isa!"

There was something about that woman that made me stutter and go bright red straight away. Perhaps it was her cool grey gaze, or possibly her posture and demeanour – stern was about right! Or maybe it was because I knew that she was a headmistress and so I felt as though I'd been sent to the principal's office. Coming across as both ignorant *and* stupid was horrible.

"It's about two girls at your school," I said quickly. "Kimmie and Pavola."

Something happened when I mentioned the names. The stern Mrs Stern suddenly looked a touch less certain. She no longer appeared to have a broomstick for a spine.

"We have no students by those names," she said. "Not now."

Like me, Kahla picked up on the implication.

"But... you did?" she said. "Once?"

"Let's go inside," Mrs Stern said, "and discuss the matter."

CHAPTER FIFTEEN

Mrs Stern

"Here they are," the headmistress said, pointing to a faded photograph in-between lots of other pictures on the wall. "Kimmie and Pavola. They were friends right from Kimmie's first day until... well, until it went wrong with Kimmie."

Kahla and I leaned forwards at the same time to get a better look and nearly banged our heads together. There they were indeed, in a line-up of boarding-school girls in grey pinafores and white shirts, looking pretty much like all the others.

Pavola was possibly prettier than most, Kimmie a little more angular. She was a skinny girl with sharp features and ordinary, wavy-brown hair.

"What went wrong?" Kahla said. "With Kimmie, I mean?"

The headmistress heaved a sigh.

"I don't suppose she ever quite settled in," she said. "She was highly able in some subjects, totally indifferent to others. I had to remind her again and again that there were certain obligations attached to her time here. She'd won a scholarship in a competition and so paid nothing to be here, the condition being that she would 'distinguish herself by diligence and hard work and serve as an example to others'. Unfortunately her behaviour wasn't always exemplary; she hated being corrected, and took great offence when I did so. She and I weren't exactly on the best of terms. And then... well, then it went very wrong. I guess it was... let me think, it was the summer poor Sniff died, so it must have been... Kimmie must have been fifteen years old. Another year and she could have left here with Oakhurst Academy's diploma, but it was not to be."

"Sniff?" Kahla said. "Who was Sniff?"

I hadn't told them that part of the dream, so maybe Kahla thought Sniff was another student. I, however, remembered only too clearly Kimmie's hatred of the little dog with its keen sense of smell. *I wish it would choke on one of its stupid bones.*

"My little dachshund," the headmistress said. "A dear friend... so sad."

"What happened to it?" I asked.

"He went missing," the headmistress said, and we could see that even now, after so many years, thinking about it still hurt. "We didn't find him until a week later, or rather, what was left of him. It must've been a fox or something. Poor little Sniff."

It was still bad, but I was relieved to hear that the dog hadn't choked on one of its bones.

"Was he your wildfriend?" Kahla asked.

"No, not... not exactly. Here at Oakhurst Academy we don't believe that students should attach themselves to a wildfriend until their own character is fully formed, but it's a rule which some students find it hard to adhere to, especially those who've already found a wildfriend before they come here. That's why very few teachers keep their own wildfriend about. We don't wish to... provoke."

I thought about Cat and felt a surge of panic. Without Cat... I wouldn't know what to do without Cat.

"Why can't you have wildfriends here?" I asked.

"Like I said... we think it's best for the students' characters to develop without such strong influence from a random animal."

A random animal! I shook my head in disbelief, I couldn't help myself. And this was supposed to be a school for wildwitches?! No wonder Shanaia had done a runner.

"So what went wrong with Kimmie?" Kahla said pointedly, to remind me and the headmistress of the real reason for our visit.

"They were only minor infractions to begin with. Food would disappear from the kitchen, and when we arranged for a guard, Kimmie was caught red-handed. Then she started bullying some of the other students into giving her their food or sweets they'd bought with their own money. She would steal fruit from the orchard, and once we even caught her having stolen, killed and plucked one of the laying hens. She was roasting it over an open fire in the forest when Sniff found her. When we asked her why she did it, she offered nothing but vague excuses, and when we pressed her, she simply said that she was hungry. But I assure you we feed our students properly here. We even got a doctor to examine her to find out what was wrong, but she was as fit as a fiddle, albeit a little underweight for her age."

My spine had started tingling, as had my tummy. *Find out who the hungry one is*, Mrs Pommerans had said. It seemed that Kimmie was hungrier than most people. And it had all started the day Pavola had shown her the cave at Westmark.

I leaned towards the picture again and studied Pavola's facial features. Didn't she remind me of someone?

"Was Pavola from Westmark?" I asked.

"Yes," the headmistress said. "What happened later was a tragedy. She and her husband lost their lives on the wildways. So terrible. And she was such a talented wildwitch."

"Did they have any children?" I asked, even though I was fairly sure I already knew the answer.

"A daughter," she said. "Shanaia Westmark. She attended this school very briefly."

Very briefly indeed, I thought, but I didn't say it out loud.

"Kimmie? Where was she from?"

"Some village near Forest Dale. Now what was the name of it? Swinstead or something like that."

"Linstead," I automatically corrected her, without knowing how.

"Yes, that's right, Linstead. Not very far from here. Well, in the end we had to expel her. It couldn't go on. I don't know what happened to her, but I suppose she went back home. Unsurprisingly, she has never shown up for school reunions."

CHAPTER SIXTEEN

The Village

Linstead was only seven or eight kilometres
from Oakhurst Academy. The headmistress offered
to lend us two of the school's riding moose, but
we settled for two bicycles instead. Star and the
riding-school horses back home were one thing,
but I seriously doubted that I was a natural-born
moose-rider.

"It's Chimera," Kahla said the moment we cycled
out through the school gate. "You know that, don't
you?"

"How's that possible?" I objected. "Surely a
revenant has to be dead and, as far as I know,
Chimera isn't."

"Are you sure?"

Strictly speaking, I couldn't be. I didn't know
what had happened to Chimera in the weeks that
had passed since I stripped her of her wings and
chased her away from Westmark.

"What words did you use to make her go away?" Kahla asked.

"Nothing special. I just told her to vanish. To go away for good." A cold thought crept under my skin. "Would that be enough to kill someone?"

Kahla pondered it. "Only if that was what you meant," she said. "Did you want her to... disappear from the surface of the earth?"

"I don't think so. I... just wanted her gone from my life. For her to leave me alone and go back to wherever she came from."

"But you didn't want her dead?"

"No!" I said. "Cross my heart!"

"It's just that there are so many coincidences..." Kahla sighed. "I mean, the girl's name is Kimmie. She knows about the cave at Westmark. And wasn't there something about her nails?"

"She liked having very long nails."

"There you go. Chimera's talons were at least ten centimetres long..."

"Yes, all right."

"So why don't we go back to Aunt Isa and tell her that?"

"Because she's busy keeping Cat alive." Not for all the world would I interrupt Aunt Isa's vital wildsong, and what if she decided that finding Chimera was more important? Nothing was more important than for Cat to live. Nothing. "And your dad. Your dad said Cat can't carry on."

"Carry on with what?"

"With..." How could I explain what Cat did? "Standing between me and... all that dead and hungry stuff in the soul tangle."

Kahla looked at me pensively.

"Is that what he's doing?"

"Yes. But it's costing him all his strength. Kahla, it's urgent!"

"But if it's that urgent, Clara... why are we on our way to some village where Chimera might have lived a million years ago?"

"Because it's important. Because..."

Because I'd felt a jolt of recognition when the headmistress mentioned the village. Because I'd known that it was called Linstead, and not Swinstead. Because I felt a tightness in my chest and a prickling behind my eyes at the very mention of the name. It had to be the place. I couldn't say exactly what we would be doing there, or why it was so important, only that it was.

Linstead appeared between meadow valleys and forested hills, and I recognized it. I'd never been there before, and yet I knew that Mrs Galli and her flock of geese lived in the little red cottage, and that at least four generations of the Barde family had lived on the farm a little further ahead.

"What is it?" Kahla wanted to know.

I'd stopped. I didn't think I could stay upright on the bike for much longer.

"Let's just walk," I said.

An old woman sat reading on a bench set against the whitewashed farmhouse wall, making the most of the sunshine. Every now and then she made a note in the margin with a stubby pencil.

"Mrs Barde?" I said, because I was fairly certain that it was her.

"Yes?" she squinted against the sunlight. "What can I do for you, girls?"

"We just wanted to know... that is, we..." I stumbled over the words, but Kahla didn't hesitate.

"We're here to find out what happened to a girl called Kimmie," she said. "We were told by Oakhurst Academy that she came from here."

Mrs Barde snapped shut her book. It was called "The Kitchen Herb Garden", I noticed.

"Why do you want to know?" she said. And she wasn't looking at Kahla, but at me.

"It's terribly important," I stammered. "Something... something disastrous might happen unless... unless we can stop it in time."

"Well, that doesn't surprise me," Mrs Barde said dryly. "Disasters have always piled up in Kimmie's wake. Come inside and have a glass of squash. Are you students at Oakhurst Academy?"

"No," Kahla said. "I study with Clara's aunt."

"I see," was all Mrs Barde said, and she asked no further questions. "Follow me. It's this way."

She brought us inside the main building's big kitchen, and fetched a jug of squash from the fridge.

"It's mostly blackcurrant," she said. "Last year's raspberries were a bit of a disappointment."

I don't know if I'd expected paraffin lamps and a woodstove, like at Aunt Isa's – perhaps I had. But here there was a fridge and a chest freezer, and a battered radio was crackling on the kitchen table because someone had turned down the volume without switching it off completely. There was checked oilcloth on the table and geraniums and white net curtains in the windows. Faded family photographs dotted with fly stains were attached to the fridge door with colourful magnets.

"My children flew the coop long ago," said Mrs Barde when she noticed me looking at them. "They can't be bothered with country life. So now it's just my husband and me. For as long as that may be."

"Kimmie?" Kahla reminded her. "We were talking about Kimmie."

"Worried I might witter on about my children and grandchildren, are you?" Mrs Barde said with a twinkle in her eye. "Relax, child. I'll stick to the matter in hand. Kimmie. Yes." She sighed – almost like the headmistress had done. "Well, she was a clever girl. Won that scholarship, got a place at Oakhurst and everything."

"We know," Kahla said impatiently. "But they threw her out, and then what happened?"

"Not much. She came home. She refused to go back to school, or maybe her dad thought enough was enough. So I guess she helped out at home and... well, nobody wanted to pry."

"Into what?" Kahla asked.

"We all knew that he was a hard man. Hard on his girls, too. They didn't have much, barely scraping by; he made his living selling firewood and doing odd jobs for people, fixing windows, building garages, that kind of thing. Sometimes he sold pheasants and game."

"The girls," I said. "There was more than one?" I knew the answer the moment I asked the question. Yes. There had been two of them. There were two sisters in that house. And they had had a swing...

"Kimmie had a sister," Mrs Barde said. "Maira. She was a few years younger. Then that awful thing happened: Maira disappeared. There was a snowstorm, a vicious blizzard, couldn't see a hand in front of your face; what the girls were doing outside in that weather, no one could understand. But when we found her three days later, she was as cold and stiff as an icicle, frozen to death, poor thing. Less than a week later Kimmie was gone, too. And we never found her."

"She... just disappeared?"

"Yes."

Kahla shifted uneasily. I didn't know if she was thinking what I was thinking, but I guessed she was. There was a dead girl in the story now. Was she the revenant?

"We had a police investigation and everything," Mrs Barde said. "But no charges were ever brought. Her father said she'd run away. And maybe she had. Who could blame her?"

"Why?"

"Like I said. He was hard on those girls. And... well, I reckon she had few friends in the village. She was a bit strange even before she went to Oakhurst Academy, and lots of people thought she was stuck up. When she came back in disgrace, as it were, people were only too ready to mock her. And then there was the petty thieving."

"She stole things?"

"Let me put it this way – no one put cakes on the windowsill to cool when she was nearby. And several of us lost chickens. Something that doesn't exactly make you popular around here..."

I sipped my squash. I didn't really know if I wanted to hear more. If Kimmie really was Chimera, then... I'd never really thought about Chimera having parents and a childhood just like everybody else. I mean, the first time I saw her she had giant wings and was covered in feathers. Back then it had been easier to imagine her hatching from an egg.

"What about her dad? And... she must have had a mum as well?"

"Oh, they still live in their cottage. But we don't see a lot of them these days."

CHAPTER SEVENTEEN

Gabriel's House

My head hurt. It felt as if the sun were boring into my eye sockets, right into my brain. The squash Mrs Barde had given us sloshed around in my tummy and gave me a strange jellyfish sensation, as if I were a sack of water with floppy arms and legs that just wanted to be carried along by the current.

"We need to stop for a minute," I said to Kahla.

"But we must be so close," she protested. "Is it urgent or isn't it? Make up your mind."

"If we don't, I'm going to throw up."

She got off her bike reluctantly. She'd actually unwound one of her scarves and tied it around her waist, but showed no other signs of feeling the heat of the sun.

We'd stopped on a road that was nothing but two cart tracks. There was forest on both sides of the road, a mixture of tall, dark pines, slender birches and something I thought was alder shrub.

The forest floor glowed green with moss and gave softly under my feet, but this only added to the discomfort – as if I weren't on firm ground.

Suddenly I felt incredibly dizzy. I clung to the handlebars with both hands, but it was no use because the bicycle fell over and I fell with it.

"Clara!"

The darkness of the pines wavered and spun above me, and I was vaguely aware of a pedal digging into my side and Kahla saying something a very long way away.

I'm tired of this, I thought. Tired of being jerked back and forth, in and out of my body as if it weren't my own, but just some random human suit I'd been handed at birth. I waited to see what would happen this time – who would I be stuffed into now? A bird, an animal, a human being? Kimmie once more?

None of the above.

I was lying on the forest floor, I could smell earth and resin, and I was still me. Still exhausted, still with a pounding headache, but I was me. And then I heard a familiar voice inside me whisper: *Mine. Keep your paws off her!*

Cat. It was Cat protecting me. It should have given me a boost, but it didn't because although he had put himself between me and the bad stuff, I could hear how weak he was. How much it cost him.

"Cat," I whispered. "Save yourself. And I'll do the same."

Kahla looked around.

"Is he here?"

"No." I didn't dare shake my head for fear the squash really would come back up. "Not really. Not... bodily."

"Are you ill?"

"My head aches." I sat up gingerly. "But apart from that... no, let's get going. But is it OK if we just push our bikes?"

"Of course. No, wait..." Kahla placed a hand on either side of my head and started humming. And the nausea actually sank back into my stomach rather than sloshing around at the back of my throat. I felt stronger and my head hurt less.

"Thank you," I said.

She just nodded.

The house, or the cottage as Mrs Barde had called it, lay in a clearing in the forest, surrounded by a collection of sheds, outhouses and log piles. A rusty green metal post box with plastic letters stuck to the side read: G BRIEL.

"There's probably an A missing," Kahla said. "But is it a first name or a surname?"

"Surname," I said, without mentioning the cold jab of recognition that had pierced me at the sight. A thin column of smoke rose from the chimney, so it seemed that someone was home.

Kahla walked resolutely up to the door and knocked.

Nothing happened. A resurrected winter fly buzzed in the sun. Apart from that it was quiet.

"Try again."

Kahla knocked on the door, a little harder this time.

Still nothing happened.

"Hello?" she shouted, way too loud, it seemed to me. "Is anybody home?"

"Shhh," I hissed. She looked at me as if I were insane, and of course I was. I mean, if you knock surely it's so people can hear that you're outside and would like to be let in? But I couldn't rid myself of the feeling that being quiet would have been wiser.

We heard footsteps coming from inside – light, but slow. Then the door was opened.

"Yes?"

She was small, scrawny and ancient. She wasn't very wrinkled, but there was something about her skin – it looked like wrapping paper that had been smoothed out and reused too many times. There was something sparrow-like about her, from the brittle-looking collarbones showing through the tired skin to the short feathery grey hair that looked as if she merely took a pair of scissors to it whenever it grew long enough to get in her way. She wore an oversized old lumberjack shirt and a pair of green gardening trousers ripped at the knees. Her face was tense and apprehensive.

"Eh..." Even Kahla didn't know what to say.

"Are you collecting for charity?" she asked. "We don't give to charity."

"No," I said. "We're not... collecting. We... we would just really like to know... like to know a bit about... a bit about Kimmie."

At first, nothing happened. It was as if the name had to work its way through her brain. Then she closed her eyes, squeezed them shut, and her whole face contracted like a fist clenching.

"We... could come back another time, if that would be more convenient..." Kahla said.

"No, we can't," I protested, thinking about Cat. "It has to be now! I'm sorry, but... are you Kimmie's mum?"

She opened her eyes again.

"Of course I am," she said. "Come in."

CHAPTER EIGHTEEN

The Jackdaw on the Perch

Kimmie's room wasn't big. Perhaps it was the sloping walls that made me think of my own room at Aunt Isa's. But there was no round window here, just an ordinary square one. The curtains might once have been floral, but they'd faded so far that the flowers were nothing but blurred pink splodges on a grey background. There was a small, white-painted writing desk below the window. The stacks of books piled up on it meant there was hardly room if you'd wanted to do any actual writing; on top of one of the stacks sat a not particularly well-stuffed jackdaw, perched on a branch with its head tilted slightly. Its beak had lost its colour and it was a bit cross-eyed. It looked incredibly dead.

There was wallpaper on the walls with a pattern that might once have matched the curtains, white with garlands of pink rosebuds surrounded by pale-green leaves, but I could hardly make it out because of the many pictures, posters, drawings and photographs, all of birds. There were crows, ravens, jackdaws, sparrows, thrushes and wood pigeons, tits and blackbirds, forest birds, waterfowl, waders, raptors, game birds... birds, birds, and more birds. A row of glass display boxes held the white wing bones from different types of bird, arranged on a background of black cardboard. Three empty bird cages were stacked in a corner and a quick look revealed that the books on the desk were pretty much all about... yes, you guessed it.

"Was she into birds?" I asked, somewhat superfluously.

"Ever since she was little," Kimmie's mum said. "She was mad about them. She could say biiiird before she could say Dad, Mum or food."

Kahla studied the cross-eyed jackdaw.

"Who made it?" she asked.

"Oh, God. That was a terrible business."

"How do you mean?"

"She'd won that grand scholarship to Oakhurst Academy. She was over the moon because the only thing she ever wanted to do was something wildwitchy, especially with birds. But I'm not sure how excited we were, my grandmother was a wildwitch, so I know a bit about it, but their dad...

well, he couldn't really see what all the fuss was about. But he did realize that Oakhurst was a posh school and that going there would ordinarily cost a lot of money."

She stopped in her tracks and stared at the jackdaw for so long I could almost believe she'd never seen it before.

"What does that have to do with the jackdaw?" I finally asked.

"Well. It was Kimmie's. It was so tame it followed her everywhere she went. But they wouldn't allow it at Oakhurst, and when she discovered that, there was a terrible fuss. Suddenly she didn't know if she wanted to go there after all, and her dad lost his temper and shouted at her, called her an ungrateful little miss and told her she was going to that school if he had to drag her there himself, she wasn't going to make a fool out of him and all those people who had given her the scholarship. Eventually, he promised he would see to it that she could take the bird with her to Oakhurst. And in the end that's what she did."

It took a while before it dawned on me what she meant. And on Kahla, I think.

"You mean... like that?" I said, pointing to the badly stuffed bird. "Dead and mounted on a twig with wire?"

She nodded. "Probably not what Kimmie had in mind," she said. "But she went without any more fuss. All quiet, which was so out of character."

All quiet. Kahla and I stared at each other, and I think we felt pretty much the same: Horror. And a stab of compassion for the girl who was once Kimmie Gabriel.

I caught myself shaking my head – not because I didn't believe the story, but because... well, because it wasn't what I wanted to hear. By now I was pretty sure that Kimmie with the tame jackdaw had turned into Chimera. And I didn't want to feel sorry for Chimera. She was evil, she was my enemy, she... she was no longer a wildwitch or a human being. She had given herself wings and feathers by stealing the lives and souls of hundreds of birds. I'd been there when the wings fell off her; I remembered the flutter of invisible wings when everything she'd stolen was set free. Somehow I'd severed her wings, even though I still didn't understand precisely how I'd done it and I very much doubted that I'd be able to do it again.

Kahla was the first to recover.

"We heard that she was expelled from Oakhurst," she said. "How did her dad react?"

Kimmie's mum hugged herself. "He got angry. But he wasn't surprised. He said he knew all along she would come to no good."

"And Kimmie? How did she take it?"

"She... she wasn't quite herself. There was something odd about her when she came home from Oakhurst. She was still interested in birds, but... I don't know. She seemed colder, somehow. I don't think she loved them any more. She once said she envied them their ability to fly. She tried to find out what made them able to do it. Studied their feathers and their skeletons, and so on." She pointed to the collection of white bird bones and the carefully drawn sketches of different types of feathers. "And then there was the food thing."

"Did she eat more than normal?" Kahla said.

"You can say that again. She was hungry all the time. Begged for food, stole it if we didn't give it to her. We had to put a lock on the door to the kitchen and to the larder, or she would creep downstairs at night and eat us out of house and home."

"And she never used to be like that?"

"No. No, she was never really interested in food until she got to Oakhurst. The strange thing was that she didn't get fat, no matter how much she ate. The opposite happened. She seemed to get thinner and thinner, and sharper and sharper to look at. At first we thought she might have worms or something, but the doctor said she didn't."

I wondered if Kimmie would have been hungry enough to try and eat new-born badger cubs. The thought intruded, even though I didn't want it to. I pushed it away with a feeling of nausea.

"Mrs Gabriel..." Kahla hesitated, which didn't seem like her. "Kimmie... had a sister, didn't she? Maira."

Kimmie's mum suddenly looked as if someone had drained the blood out of her and replaced it with lead. No, not suddenly. She seemed to have grown heavier and greyer while we'd been talking about Kimmie. However, when Kahla mentioned Maira, the last trace of life disappeared from her face.

"You have to go now," she said. "I don't know why you've come here... asking all these questions, but you have to go now. I thought... I thought you might know where Kimmie was, but you're no different from all the other snoopers..."

She broke off. For a moment she stood completely still. Then she made a strange, clutching movement with one hand as if clinging to something no one else could see. Whatever it was, she missed it. She staggered forwards, slumped to her knees and ended up sitting on the floor, leaning against what was once Kimmie's bed.

Kahla and I both froze. Back home, a teacher had once collapsed during a German lesson and been taken away in an ambulance because he had had what they called "a funny turn", but I hadn't been there when it happened, I'd only seen the ambulance drive off with him. I wasn't even sure you could call an ambulance out here, let alone what number to ring. Nor did I know if Kimmie's mum was having a funny turn, but she certainly didn't look too good.

"Mrs Gabriel?" Kahla ventured cautiously. "Is something wrong?"

Which was a pretty stupid thing to say because something obviously had to be wrong for her to slide onto the floor in that jellyfish way.

At first Kimmie's mum didn't say anything. Her eyes were open, but I had the feeling she wasn't really looking at anything.

Kahla squatted down in front of her and clasped both her hands. I heard her take a deep breath before she started singing a slightly hesitant wildsong.

It did have an effect, but not the one we had been hoping for. With great effort, Mrs Gabriel snatched back her hands and snarled at Kahla:

"No. Not that. Blasted witchery."

"But... I think I can help..."

"No. Go away," she groaned. "Pills!"

"Where, Mrs Gabriel?" I asked.

"Bathroom. Cabinet."

I stared wildly at Kahla.

"Stay with her," I said. "And if she passes out, please will you...?"

"Not really," Kahla said, looking frustrated. "I can't. Not when she's made it clear she doesn't want me to."

I went out into the passage and opened the next door. It wasn't the bathroom, but another girl's bedroom, Maira's, I presumed. I didn't have time to take a proper look, although my curiosity pricked me, so I only caught a brief glimpse of sunshine-yellow walls, a massive pile of stuffed toys and posters of cute baby animals with very big eyes.

The bathroom was the next door. I found two different types of pills and filled a toothbrush mug with water.

Fortunately, Mrs Gabriel hadn't passed out when I came back. In fact, she looked a little better. She shook a pill out of one glass bottle and popped it in her mouth, but she didn't want the water.

"No," she said, her voice a little thick due to the pill. "I'm not supposed to swallow it. I just leave it under the tongue to dissolve."

"Is there someone we can get for you?" Kahla asked. "How about Mr Gabriel?"

Kimmie's mum ran a trembling hand through her tousled, grey hair. Her brow furrowed.

"I don't understand why he's not back yet," she said. "He was only going out to have a look at it and take some samples, and it isn't that far."

"Look at what, Mrs Gabriel?"

"Some kind of disease."

How could you have a look at a disease?

"What kind of disease?"

"The trees. Well, pretty much everything. He thinks there's something wrong with the soil. He did report it to the Forestry Commission, but they didn't do much, so he decided to take some soil samples himself and have them analysed. He says it's spreading."

A knot tightened in my stomach.

"What's happening to the trees?" I asked.

"They're dying. Everything is, he says. It's spreading quickly. It's a bit eerie – there's this dead spot where nothing lives now."

Kahla and I looked at each other.

"So... where would we find this spot?" Kahla asked.

CHAPTER NINETEEN

The Dead Forest

A forest is noisy. There's always something rustling, creaking, squeaking or scolding. If you're having a picnic, you might think of the forest as quiet and peaceful, but from a wildwitch's point of view, it's one of the busiest places in the world. It's like the main railway station in a big city, a teeming, buzzing melting pot of plants and animals, of life.

Imagine standing in the middle of the arrivals hall at such a station. A place where there ought to be people everywhere, schoolchildren, office workers, pensioners and housewives, young women and grumpy old men, kids screaming for ice-cream, pickpockets, backpackers, noisy loud-speakers, cleaners with humming floor sweepers, the smell of deep fat fryers in burger bars, bottles clattering, wheeled suitcases, beeping, noise, noise, noise.

Imagine being in a place like that, and it's quiet.

Completely quiet.

Not a sound, not a single footstep, no shouting or laughing, nothing.

There's not a soul to be seen. There are no smells, not even of pee.

That was the dead forest.

Kahla had stopped. I heard her swallow a mouthful of saliva – it was that quiet.

"What happened here?" she whispered.

"I think everything's been eaten," I said.

It had got worse since the last time I saw it, when I borrowed the hawk's eyes. The dead trees and their bare branches were the first thing I noticed, surrounded as they were by buds and spring green. Some had already collapsed, snapped as if their sturdy trunks were nothing but matches, or uprooted. The pale, dead roots resembled crooked fingers still trying to cling on to something although it was far too late.

I saw them first because they were the biggest, but everything else had gone too – tender anemone shoots, new wood sorrel, shrubs and mosses, beetles, snails, mushrooms on old tree stumps, the ants on the forest floor. The spring wind no longer played with grasses and leaves, but whirled up layers of thick grey and brown dust that covered the earth like the ashes after a fire.

Kahla was about to take a step forwards, but I stopped her.

"Don't go in there," I said, grabbing her arm before she reached the dust. "It'll eat you too."

Kahla frowned. I could see that she was starting to recover from the shock. I prayed she wouldn't rush in despite my warning, believing that a skilled wildwitch could handle anything.

"But standing here doesn't solve anything," she objected.

"Kahla. This isn't something you and I can fix," I said. "The smartest thing we can do is call for help as quickly and as loudly as we can. We've found the hungry one. That's what we came to do."

"No, to find out who the hungry one was," Kahla corrected me. "That was what Mrs Pommerans said."

"But we know that as well. The hungry one is Kimmie. And Kimmie is Chimera."

The moment I uttered the name, we heard a sound. A strangled cry in the middle of the great silence.

"Here..." it said. "Here..."

"That's a man," Kahla said.

"Yes. It must be Kimmie's dad. Mr Gabriel."

"Well, then at least he hasn't been eaten," Kahla declared.

We hurried through the living forest towards the shouting. I noticed that Kahla was careful to stay clear of the crumbling tree trunks and the grey dust.

"Over here..." the cry sounded again. It was a man, and yet there was something wrong with his voice. Somehow it sounded... withered.

"There!" Kahla said, pointing. "By the pine tree."

The man – Kimmie's dad – was lying face-down on the ground. His black, red and white lumberjack shirt was like a signal flag, so we knew immediately that this was a human being. After all, not many animals wore plaid.

He had stopped shouting. Perhaps he could hear that we were on our way.

"Mr Gabriel?" Kahla said. "What's wrong?"

He didn't say very much. Kahla knelt down beside him, but despite us having found him, he didn't stop trying to crawl across the ground, dragging his legs behind him.

"Stop," Kahla said. "If you lie still, I'll try to help you. You'll only wear yourself out."

He let out some slurred sounds that were barely words. He seemed to have trouble controlling his tongue.

"Isummin," he said. "Isummin. Hun!"

Hun? I couldn't see any vicious barbarian hordes descending on us; he must mean something else.

Again Kahla tried to stop him, but though his legs didn't work, he still had strength left in his arms. He pushed her and her helping hands aside violently.

"Hun," he said again. "Hun. Hun. Hun."

There was quite a lot of grey in his dark hair, and he had lines around his eyes and mouth, but I could tell just from looking that he regarded himself as a strong man, and that that made it worse. He wasn't used to being helpless. I could see from the trail behind him on the forest floor how he had pulled himself along on his stomach and elbows. Grey dust stuck to the upturned soles of his feet.

"Kahla," I whispered. "Look at his legs."

It had started at his feet, but it was creeping up his shins. It wasn't just "grey dust", as I'd first thought. It was... no, alive was completely the wrong word. But it was moving. It was spreading. It was eating its way through his legs, one bite at a time.

His sturdy boots were falling apart, and only a few fraying grey cobwebs were left of what had once been his socks. But the most shocking thing lay underneath. His skin was also grey. I don't just mean pale, I mean grey. It cracked and it split, and the cracks bubbled like acid. Flakes of skin fell off in front of our eyes, then they crumbled and turned into grey dust.

"Isummin," he groaned again. "Isummin. Hun!"

At long last I realized what he was trying to say. His mouth and his tongue would no longer obey him, the air hissed out of him without turning into sharp, clear consonant sounds such as C and T and R.

It's coming. It's coming. Run.

"Kahla," I said. "He's telling us something is coming. That we need to run. Now!"

But by then, of course, it was already too late.

CHAPTER TWENTY

Inside the Monster

It's difficult to describe the monster.

If I were to say "dragon", most people would have a mental image of scales and claws and a long reptilian body, maybe wings and a bit of smoke seeping out of the nostrils: a dragon. They don't exist, at least not in the real world, and yet we all know what they look like.

This was no dragon.

It was... it kept changing. I didn't know what to call it. It had a kind of skin, but one that bubbled and burst and shifted shape. Things stuck out of it. Stones. Leaves. Small animals and insects, beetles, worms, a bird, the outline of a lizard. But not the same things every time. They seemed to rise up and then sink back down, as if the skin weren't skin, but... I don't know. Lava, perhaps. Solid yet liquid at the same time. Eyes. Eyes would pop up, not just in the part I thought of as its head, but everywhere. A

hand. A wing. A pine cone. The skull of a mole. As if it made no difference, everything could be eaten, everything could be devoured, used, drained of life.

A sudden, absurd memory of a healthy eating poster flashed through my mind: *You are what you eat*. But the thing that came stumbling, tumbling, falling through the forest had devoured so much that everything bulged, swelled and protruded before being sucked in again.

Someone screamed. I think it must have been Kahla because I was completely dumb with horror.

Everything it touched died on the spot. One moment a young birch tree was standing with tiny, luminous, green buds, the next it was reduced to a grey silhouette before collapsing soundlessly into a pile of grey dust. A long-tailed field mouse hesitated before trying to run away. Its fur dropped off in front of our eyes, then its skin and muscles; I swear it happened so quickly that the skeleton was still moving a split second before it was gobbled up. A few mouse bones stuck out of the bubbling skin, a tail dangled briefly from one shoulder.

I don't know how big it was. Perhaps it had no size at all. It grew enormous when it swallowed up the birch, but seemed to contract when taking the mouse. It was neither fast nor slow. It stopped, quivering and wobbling slightly, before suddenly rolling forwards, looming above our heads like one of those tsunamis I'd seen on TV.

Kahla had grabbed Mr Gabriel's arm and was trying to drag him away. She was screaming and shouting for me to take his other arm.

I stood rooted.

I don't know if I thought anything at all. All I could feel was how the sparrow's heart had beaten and then broken. I remembered the hunger of the grass snake. The smell of fresh squirrel blood and Martin's grandmother, soaked to the skin. And I remembered Cat.

Then I raised both arms above my head, clenched my fists and crossed my wrists.

"S

 T

 O

 P."

It was more than a shout. More than wildsong. It was a wall, a wall that was just as tall as the thing. The monster.

There was a place deep inside me. A place where it was enough. A place as hard as flint or granite, and just as tough to shift.

I hadn't known that it was there. But when I said go away and I meant it, it came from that place. And when I ordered it to stop, then it did.

Kahla stopped with her mouth open, and both hands around Mr Gabriel's upper arm. He stopped in the middle of his attempt to escape. And the thing stopped too.

Not one more mouse, not one more sparrow.

I stared up at the monster. It had a face, I could see it now that the thing was no longer bulging and bubbling quite as much. The eyes were where eyes were supposed to be, something reminiscent of a nose, a gaping hole that had once been a mouth. In the worst possible way it was the face of Chimera, but at the same time... it wasn't. Dead flakes of dust and skin scattered over its chest – over *her* chest – and turned into ash-grey powder, but somewhere inside it was alive.

"Chimera."

The eyes flickered, squinted, bulged as if she were struggling to keep control of the head. Eventually they settled and focused on me like the crosshairs of two gun sights.

"Wit... ch child..."

It wasn't until she said it, not until the thick, almost unrecognizable sound emerged from her mouth, that I was sure. It *was* her. Behind the bubbling skin and the swollen, mutating monster body, something still recognized me, something that was still her. Hatred flared up in her yellow predator's eyes.

I'd made her stop, but she wouldn't let herself be held back for very long. Soon she would roll on and if I touched her, I would be crushed and swallowed up like everything else, like everyone else. My heart would break as the sparrow's had done, with the wet, red sound it made when you squash a berry.

Some enemies can't be vanquished from the outside.

Suddenly I found myself clutching Mrs Pommerans's small, round box. Just a tiny bit, she had said, but something told me that a tiny bit wouldn't be enough, not now, not here. I twisted the lid off the tin and flung it up in the air between the Chimera monster and me. The fine, green dream dust scattered to all sides, and we found ourselves inside a luminous green powder-cloud.

I guess I'd expected the vademecum powder to knock Chimera out. Mrs Pommerans had stressed that it wasn't a sleeping potion, but a small pinch of it had made me dream a very useful dream, so I had high hopes as I flung the whole box in her face.

Not in my wildest dreams had I imagined what would happen the moment the fine, green dust started falling on top of Kahla, the man on the ground, Chimera – and me.

CHAPTER TWENTY-ONE

Grey Snow

Snow covered everything. It was grey rather than white and it reminded me of dust, but it was cold and it melted when it came into contact with the skin. I held up my hand and caught a few flakes.

I was alone. And that made it difficult. I studied the hand that had caught the snowflake. A human hand. At least I hadn't turned into a sparrow or a grass snake. But was I still Clara? It was hard to decide when there was no one around to tell me who I was.

I felt like Clara, but then again, I had done so during the dream when I was really Kimmie.

I didn't like the wobbly sensation it gave me. I looked down at myself, thinking: if I'm wearing Clara's clothes, then surely I must be her?

At first I thought they were my clothes. Clara's, I mean. Then I started to have doubts. I wasn't wearing the jeans I thought I'd put on that morning, and... or wait. Was I? It was as if they'd changed colour in front of my very eyes. To begin with they'd seemed grey, now they were blue.

Do you even know who you are, little witch?

I looked around frantically. It sounded like... it was Cat. And yet his voice was strangely alien. And he had never called me "little witch" before.

Do you become Clara when you wear Clara's clothes? Or because other people tell you you're Clara?

"Oh, stop it," I said. "You know exactly what I mean."

Do I? He got up and slowly licked the snow off a front paw. *If you're not careful, you'll end up like The Nothing.*

I was about to ask him what he meant, but I didn't because I knew exactly what he meant. The Nothing didn't know who she was. She'd follow anyone who would tell her, even Chimera. If Chimera told her she was nothing, then she was nothing.

"I'm not The Nothing," I whispered with a cold and bitter taste of grainy snow on my tongue.

Then who are you? Clara Mouse? Mummy's little Mousie?

"It's just a nickname," I protested, yet I could feel how it diminished me. Small, scared and cautious. "Why are you being like this?"

But it was as if the drifting snow blew the question right back into my face: why are you being like this? And suddenly Cat had disappeared. Once more I was alone in the grey snow, getting colder and colder, and starting to wonder if he had even been here in the first place or whether it was all in my mind.

"It was just something you imagined," I told myself firmly. It was a dream. It wasn't snowing. There was nothing here but illusion and imagination.

I couldn't see much apart from snow. It blew into my face, it stuck to my clothes so that soon it didn't matter if my trousers were grey or blue; it covered everything around me, leaving only blurred outlines of objects under the snow. Was that a bush or a log pile? A tree or a street lamp? It was impossible to tell.

"Where am I?" I asked, not knowing if anyone could hear me or would reply if they could. "Where has all that snow come from?"

It's Kimmie's snow, said the voice that was no longer wholly Cat's. *Somewhere inside her it's always snowing.*

Kimmie's snow? What was that supposed to mean?

"Kimmie!"

Someone was shouting in the snowstorm and yet again I had this wobbly sensation. Was I meant to reply? Was it me she was looking for?

"Kimmie, where are you? Kimmiiiiiie!"

It was the voice of a frightened and lonely younger sister, and I felt compelled to answer whether or not I was Kimmie. She had been calling for so long; I could hear it in her raw and frozen voice.

Then I spotted her. She was heading towards me, but she didn't seem to see me.

"Kimmiiiiie!" she called out again.

"I don't think she's here," I said, though I wasn't sure.

She didn't hear me. She walked right past me, a pale, shivering girl with a grey scarf wrapped four times around her neck and the dots of snowflakes on her dark-grey, woolly hat.

"Where are you," she said, but it was barely a question now. She was so tired she was dragging her feet, and she didn't have the energy to carry on searching. She stopped a short distance from me and sat down abruptly in the snow.

"Don't do that," I said with a budding realization that this was dangerous. "Don't go to sleep." Wasn't that what they said? That was how you froze to death; it started with you feeling sleepy. You didn't suffer; you just slept right into your death.

And suddenly I remembered Mrs Barde's words: *Cold and stiff as an icicle, frozen to death, poor thing.*

She still couldn't hear me. She sat in the snow, rocking back and forth, her shoulders pulled up around her ears and her arms folded across her chest, right up under her chin.

"Kimmiiiiiee..." It was no longer a cry; it was a quiet, abandoned whimper. I took a step forwards. She couldn't hear or see me. I wondered if she would be able to feel it if I put my hand on her shoulder?

"Maira!"

I spun around. Behind me, Kimmie came walking, the real Kimmie, I recognized her from the boarding school picture. She wasn't wearing a hat or a scarf, not even a jacket, only a pair of too-short pyjama bottoms and a T-shirt with birds printed on it, black and white and grey, against a white background. Her bare legs were stuck into a pair of wellies and she'd wrapped an old potato sack around her shoulders like a shawl, presumably to stay warm. Despite her inadequate clothing she wasn't nearly as frozen as Maira. Just angry.

"What are you doing here? Did he throw you out, too?"

"Kimmie!" Maira staggered to her feet and threw her arms around her sister. "I couldn't find you. I looked and looked, but you weren't anywhere."

"Did he throw you out, too?" Kimmie said again, still very angry.

"Who? Dad? Of course not. I went outside to look for you. Here... I brought you this." She rummaged around her pockets and found a few slices of bread and a small packet of something.

"Give it to me!" Kimmie practically snatched the bread from her hands and stuffed it into her mouth.

"Don't you want to make a sandwich?" Maira sounded perplexed.

But Kimmie had already swallowed the bread and was busy tearing open the tinfoil. It looked like it held slices of salami, but I barely had time to see before Kimmie wolfed them down.

"Don't you have anything else?" she asked sharply.

"No," Maira said. "Yes, I had an apple as well, but I... I ate it. I didn't mean to."

"You ate it? Maira, you brat!"

Maira flinched as if Kimmie had slapped her.

"I've been walking for hours..." she said. "I got hungry..."

"Maira, I'm sorry..." Kimmie pressed both hands against her mouth as if wanting to push the words back inside. "I didn't mean it. Please don't be upset. It's just that... I'm so hungry. You can't imagine how hungry I am. And last night when I went to help myself to a little bread, just a little... he was there, waiting for me. Telling me I'd stolen food for the last time. And then he threw me out. Into the snowstorm. I walked to Linstead, but they chased me away, too, or at least Mr Barde did, he's still mad about his hens. So I didn't know where else to go. And then it started to snow. And I was so hungry."

"Come home with me," Maira said.

"He won't let me in."

"Oh, yes, he will. Kimmie, he definitely will. He was probably just trying to frighten you." Maira placed her hand on Kimmie's arm.

Kimmie looked down at her sister's hand. She sniffed. First just a quick sniff, then she inhaled the girl's scent with a violent snort. A tremor went through her, all the way from the soles of her feet to the top of her head.

Then she suddenly retreated five or six stumbling steps in the snow.

"Kimmie, what is it?"

"Stay away from me."

"Kimmie!"

"Thanks for the food. Now go home."

"I don't think I know the way..."

"Maira. Get lost. Miserable little brat, do as you're told!"

Maira started to cry. She was scared. So was I. Because I recognized the black hunger in Kimmie's eyes, I recognized that sniffing, like an animal searching for food. For life.

"Run, Maira..." I whispered, although I knew she couldn't hear me.

And she did. She didn't fully grasp the expression in Kimmie's eyes, but it frightened her. She turned around and ran on stiff, tired legs and Kimmie buried her face in her hands and she too wept loudly, heaving sobs of the kind that hurt all the way up the throat.

At first I was relieved that Maira had got away. Then I remembered the ending: she never made it home. They found her, cold and stiff as an icicle. If Kimmie had known that, she would probably have cried even louder.

"Do you think you know everything now?"

The voice behind me was colder than the snow. Kimmie dissolved in front of my eyes as if she were a slide projection someone had turned off.

Chimera was standing behind me. She had no wings; I had taken them from her. But nor was she the swollen monster from the dead forest. She looked like Kimmie more than ever, and of course I had already worked out that Kimmie was Chimera, or at least I knew the beginning of her story.

My heart pounded against my ribs, thud, thud, thud, hard like a hammer. Chimera's yellow eyes. Chimera's long talons. Exactly the kind you encounter in a nightmare. Only I had a creeping, worrying sensation that this nightmare wasn't mine. It was *Kimmie's* snow. *Chimera's* bad dream. But it was still just a dream. Wasn't it?

"This is a dream," I said hesitantly. "You can't hurt me here."

Her sharp predator's face lit up in something that was definitely not a smile.

"Oh, is that what you think?" she said.

CHAPTER TWENTY-TWO

Revenge

"You took my wings," Chimera said. "What do you think I should take from you in return?"

"Nothing," I whispered. I couldn't move. I hadn't been able to for some time. Without me noticing, my legs had turned to ice. I don't mean that I was really cold. I mean they really had turned into ice – hard, grey, cloudy ice that wouldn't budge. "Those wings never belonged to you. You took life – you stole life – to get them."

It was as if she hadn't heard me. There was dense snow all around us – in the air, on the ground; it covered an indeterminate landscape of something that might or might not be bushes and trees. Everything was snow. Kimmie's snow. Chimera's snow.

"I could take... this one."

Lightly, she touched what I'd taken to be a tree stump. The snow lifted, whirled around as if she'd blown it away, and settled elsewhere. The tree stump was Kahla. She was sitting on the ground with her knees pulled right up to her chin, and she, too, had feet and legs of ice.

"Clara..." she whimpered. "I'm fr-eeezing."

Poor Kahla. More than anything she hated being cold. But this wasn't real, I reminded myself. I looked at Chimera.

"This is just a dream," I said. "You can't hurt Kahla here."

"Are you sure?" Chimera said. "Are you quite sure about that?"

She touched Kahla again, and the ice ate its way up another part of the sitting Kahla figure.

Dream-Kahla screamed. And she sounded exactly like real-life Kahla.

"Leave her alone," I said. "She's never done anything to you!"

"No," Chimera said. "But it's usually the innocent who suffer. Or die..."

Was she thinking of Maira? Perhaps she was. For a brief moment she looked more like Kimmie than she usually did.

"Or what about this one?" she said, touching something that looked like a snow-covered log pile. "He's not particularly innocent."

It was Martin. Martin the Meanie in his hospital bed with tubes and cannulas and machines. He wasn't unconscious now, he could see me and he frantically shook his head as if that were the only body part he could move.

"Let me go," he shouted in a hoarse, sandpapery voice. "Let me go, you cow, or I'll beat the..." It wasn't clear if he was talking to me or Chimera, but he was looking at me.

"We could do without him, couldn't we?" Chimera said. "Now what is it you call him at school – Martin the Meanie?"

How did she know that? It felt as if she could look right inside my head and help herself to whatever she wanted – everything I knew, everything I remembered, everything I'd ever dreamt.

"No," I said. "Don't take him either."

Because while I was fairly sure that Kahla was safe, that even if dream-Kahla got hurt, then real-life Kahla wouldn't be... while I could just about believe that... I didn't dare believe that Martin would survive in the real world. He was part of the soul tangle and the thread that connected him to life was now so fragile I could almost hear the delicate, high-pitched whine it would make if you pulled it so hard it snapped.

"Or I could take this one, but I don't suppose you care about him, so he doesn't count..."

It was Mr Gabriel. Kimmie's dad.

He was lying on the ground as he had done in real life, dragging his useless legs behind him, but he stared up at her with a defiant iciness that was just as strong as hers.

"You don't scare me," he said.

"Don't I? Do you even know what I'm capable of now? I'm no longer that powerless little girl you could send to bed without her supper. Or scold. Or lock out."

"Someone's feeling sorry for themselves, eh?" His voice was like a knife. "Poooor little Kimmie."

The sting hit home. I could tell from the way she flinched, and the strangely surprised expression in her eyes.

"Shut your mouth," she said. "That's not my name any more."

"You have the name I gave you," he said. "No matter what you call yourself to make yourself sound important, you are and always will be Kimmie Gabriel!"

Every time he called her Kimmie, something happened to her. Her face grew younger and more vulnerable. Not as sharp, pointy and predatory as the Chimera I knew.

"Shut up," she said with fading strength and a shrill, strained quality to her voice.

He tried to sit up.

"Stay where you are," she ordered, but he ignored her.

"Little Kimmie always had to show off," he said. "Little Kimmie always wanted to be special. Little Kimmie, who was so smart she could do without her head."

"Stop it!"

He was standing up now.

"What are you going to do, little Kimmie? What *can* you do? Useless little Miss I'm-so-Special."

Was he out of his mind? Why bait her? He, too, was in a pitiful state in the real world, and I had a strong hunch that she could kill him if she wanted to.

She grimaced.

"Perhaps I should stuff you and put you on a twig," she said. "See how you like that!"

He frowned.

"Are you still sulking about that?" he said. "It was just a scruffy old bird."

Chimera contracted her talons, and invisible hands seemed to lift Mr Gabriel's long body into the air.

"He wasn't a scruffy old bird," she said. "He was my friend. And you took him. And you wrung his neck. Cut him open. Skinned him. Stuffed him with sawdust. And put him on that ridiculous twig..."

Her father's neck twitched. The invisible hands spun him around and turned him inside out. In a few seconds his insides had disappeared as if they were never there in the first place, and his skin and hair and clothes were forced over a framework only roughly human-shaped. Sawdust spilled from his mouth and ears, and his hands looked like washing-up gloves stuffed with cotton wool.

This is a dream, I kept telling myself. A dream, a dream, a dream... It had to be because although there was nothing left of him but his skin, he was still alive, his eyes flickered, his hollow lips tried to form the word:

"Himmie..."

A stuffed human being still able to talk.

"Shut up," she said. "Now you shut up!"

Coarse stitches sprung up across his mouth as his lips were sewn together with big black crosses like something out of a grotesque cartoon. His eyes twitched, his head jerked a little, and sawdust trickled out between the stitches, but he could no longer speak. The sound still coming from him was so strangled that it was nothing but hissing filtered through sawdust.

"Now perhaps we can get some peace around here," Chimera said. She paused with her fingertips pressed against her sharp cheekbones. "You told me yourself," she said to her stuffed dad. "Never be sentimental, you said. And I guess you were right. Caring so much about a scruffy old bird was stupid. I never made that mistake again."

She turned to me. Her yellow eyes studied me as if she were looking for the right place to stab. And there was no escape.

The dream dust had been a mistake. A terrible mistake. In the real world you could at least run away. Here inside Chimera's personal nightmare, she was far, far too strong.

I wondered if I could wake up. Would that be a way out?

I couldn't move enough to pinch my arm, my shoulders felt locked in place. So I dug my nails into my palms as viciously as I could – if pain was the trigger, that ought to work too.

Nothing happened. Nothing except for the twinge in my palms.

"What are you doing, witch child? Are you trying to get away?"

"Yes," I said defiantly. "Why not? This is a dream and I can wake up."

"And you think you'll wake up because your hand hurts a bit? It takes a lot more, trust me."

She never even touched me. She just trailed a long talon in an arc through the air. There was an icy chainsaw whine from my wrist. When I looked down, my left hand was lying on the ground. There was no blood; it looked like something that had fallen off a statue. But it was my hand.

"Did that hurt?" she asked.

"Yes," I whispered. The tears froze to ice on my lashes and made them stick together. It hurt. I'd never tried losing my hand in real life, so I didn't know whether it hurt more or less than in the dream. It burnt and throbbed, but I was still here. Pain wasn't the way out.

"You'll stay here for as long as I do," she said. "And if we wait long enough, our bodies will wither, and then you'll die, witch child. In real life as well. Get it? I hold your life in my hands. Do you understand?"

I nodded silently.

"Right, then let's negotiate, witch child. The price of a pair of wings. You didn't want to sacrifice your little wildwitch friend, nor that unpleasant young man in the bed. The scarecrow doesn't count; he's mine, not yours. So what's it to be? You *will* pay for what you have done to me. The only thing we're haggling over is the price. Oh, wait. I think I've decided."

The snow in front of me lifted, at first just a little, then a bit more. Something was lying underneath it – a flat, extended body, trapped and frozen in mid-leap.

Cat.

Ice crystals glistened in his fur. He was frozen from the tip of his nose to the end of his tail, but his golden eyes flashed with life. And with rage.

My heart skipped a beat. Not Cat. She had better keep her talons off him, I wouldn't... She mustn't...

Somewhere out there, in real life, he was lying in his basket while Aunt Isa fought to keep his limp, lifeless body alive. It wouldn't take much to snuff out his faint heartbeat, his rasping breath. She could kill him by snapping her fingers. And I could tell from the expression in her eyes that she knew it.

"Not. Cat." I could barely get the words out.

"No? I could see to it that you got to keep him forever... I think he would look nice on your mantelpiece. I promise you, he'll turn out better than my poor, ugly jackdaw."

"Don't. You. Dare. Touch. Him." Why was it so difficult to make the words? Was it because the ice was creeping closer to my heart, closer to my cold lips? "Take me. If you. Absolutely. Have. To. Take someone. Then take. Me."

She smiled bitterly.

"That wouldn't be any fun," she said. "Not here. I can't even use your blood, you don't have any." She pointed to the statue hand that was slowly being covered by falling snow. "It doesn't even hurt now, does it?"

It didn't. She'd chopped off my hand, and I could no longer feel it.

"But that." She jabbed my chest with a sharp, cold finger. "In there. That's where it hurts, isn't it? If I take your cat, it's going to hurt – isn't it?"

I couldn't speak. It hurt so much that I couldn't even nod.

"Now that would be a revenge that would satisfy the hunger – at least for a little while," she said, sounding pleased with herself.

I couldn't let her do it. But how could I fight back when I couldn't move and could barely speak?

Find out who the hungry one is.

"Kimmie."

She jumped.

"That's not my name."

"But it. Was. Once. Kimmie."

Every time I said it, my lips grew warmer.

"Kimmie, Kimmie, Kimmie..." I whispered. Was that why Mrs Pommerans had insisted it was so important? *You can't vanquish something before you've found it. And you can't find it until you know what it is.* Did I know Chimera well enough by now?

"Do you want me to stitch your lips together too?" she said.

"You take, Kimmie," I said. "All you ever do is take. What makes you think you can just take whatever you want?"

"Because I have nothing," she said. "Everything I had, I *had* to take, and I could never hold on to it; someone would always snatch it away from me. Always. My dad. That stupid school. The Raven Mothers. You. But I swear that you'll pay for this. Because when you have nothing, you have nothing to lose."

Suddenly I could see it. The hunger. It sat inside her like a black creature, a darkness, an emptiness. An empty void that could swallow up the whole world without ever being filled. And Kimmie didn't care. She didn't care if the whole world disappeared. Why should she; it wasn't her world.

I think it was the first time I understood Chimera. Understood what it must be like to be her. And I didn't like it.

At that moment a jangling, quivering sound penetrated the snow. Chimera... No, Kimmie. Kimmie clutched her heart.

"You have me."

A girl came walking through the snowdrifts. She wore a grey woolly hat and a scarf wrapped four times around her neck.

Kimmie clasped her chest as if her heart would jump out if she didn't stop it.

"You died," she said. "They took you from me. You too."

"No," Maira said. "I'm right here."

The black hunger twisted. It seeped out between Kimmie's fingers and spread across her chest.

Suddenly I remembered what Aunt Isa had said that terrible dark and hungry night where I had tried... when I had wanted to...

The hunger doesn't belong to you.

What if it didn't belong to Kimmie either?

It had taken up residence in her the day Pavola had shown her the cave. From that day onwards she had eaten and eaten, taken and taken – first to sate a simple hunger, a hunger for food. But later she had taken not only food but lives – and more and more of them.

Kimmie could feel it now. And I realized she wasn't trying to contain her heart, but her hunger. She tried, but she couldn't. It oozed out like oil between her fingers, trickling over her chest, her body, her legs.

"Go away," she screamed to Maira. "Run. I can't hold it."

The hunger was the revenant. And the revenant wasn't Chimera. Who it was or who it had been,

I didn't know. The oily, all-consuming shadow trying to escape from Chimera's chest had no face, no body, but I remembered its strength only too well. I staggered backwards on stiff ice legs, not wanting to touch the shadow *or* Chimera, I just wanted to get away.

"Help her," Maira pleaded. "She can't do it on her own."

Chimera had said it herself: *You'll stay here for as long as I do.* But what if she... was no longer here?

It was as if everything stopped for a moment. I felt the cold, the grey snowflakes that were still falling. The snow had already covered Kahla up again, and Mr Gabriel's clumsy, stuffed figure was also nearly hidden. But Cat... Cat had fought to get back on his feet, although I could see and feel that every movement threatened to burst his heart. He looked at me with eyes glowing like liquid gold.

You have claws, wildwitch. Use them.

Could I?

There was something inside me. I'd felt it before. There was something sharp and steely and once I'd used it to cut off Chimera's wings as if with an invisible sword.

I closed my eyes. I can do this, I whispered to myself and tried to believe it. I'm a wildwitch. I have claws. I'm not a little mouse. I reached for the invisible sword inside me, I stretched out my hands –

No. One was lying in the snow. Chimera had chopped it off without batting an eyelid. With only a thought. By flicking her little finger. What could I do against something that was stronger than her? How can you have claws when you don't even have two hands?

If you can't do it, then I'll die, Cat said.

It wasn't an accusation or a threat. He was just stating a fact. If I couldn't do it, that was the end. He would be gone. And the thought was unbearable. I had to, it was that simple. With one hand or with two. With or without claws, with or without invisible swords.

I opened my eyes again.

One hand was the same as it always was. The other was made of fire. I had fingers of flame, claws of fire. The heat from it rose up my arm.

I didn't shout **STOP** or **goaway**, I just thrust my flame-hand into Chimera's chest, where the revenant's hungry shadow was pouring out of her.

Ice and fire clashed in a hiss of steam. Chimera screamed. Her claws sank into my arm, but she wasn't trying to push it away, on the contrary. She pressed my flame-hand against her heart as if her only wish were to make it stop beating.

The world splintered. It was as if we'd all been inside a snow globe that someone had now smashed. Sunlight poured in, darkness, warmth, earth and sounds exploded around me.

Then it felt as if the earth rose up and hit me from behind.

Cat! I could no longer shout it out loud, but nor could I stop myself from trying.

Here, was all he said, and he was next to me, his warm, black fur, his claws and his body, and the hole in my heart was filled.

CHAPTER TWENTY-THREE

When Something Has Died

I lay still for a while.

Nothing could be wrong as long as I could feel the heat from Cat's body and hear him purr. Or at least that was how it felt. But then I sensed something else.

Underneath me the earth was moving.

Not violently and quickly as I imagined an earthquake would feel, but quietly and calmly. I was raised up and then lowered down again, as if lying on a lilo floating on gently lapping waves.

I opened my eyes just as a warm breeze rose and fluttered the leaves on the trees.

Leaves on the trees.

I had to shut my eyes and open them again. It was no use – I was still seeing the same thing. Everything was green. Including all the things that had been dead earlier. It wasn't just a fine light-green veil of spring buds, it was *green*. Everything was in bloom.

And everything was moving, very softly, very gently, in tune with the slow, gentle rhythm of the Earth.

The Earth was breathing.

"It's gone," Kahla said.

She was sitting on the grass next to me.

"Are you OK?" I couldn't help asking.

"Yes. I had some strange, cold dreams, but..." she shuddered. "Everything's fine now." She smiled. "The monster has gone, and everything's... fine."

It wasn't like her to just sit still and smile in a vaguely silly way. But I could feel it myself. You couldn't help but be happy. Happy and strangely blissful.

"I think it's the air," Kahla said. "It's almost... green."

And it was. If I looked very carefully, I could make out a soft green glow in the air around us.

Cat slowly got up and stretched every muscle in his black, feline body. He sniffed the green air. His tail swished from side to side; I think he was checking to see if there was any danger nearby. Then he sat down again and started giving himself a proper morning wash from his chin down to his tummy, then all four paws and as much of his back as he could reach.

I raised my hands from my lap and studied them. There were two of them. They looked normal, apart from... I pushed my watch up my arm. I had a thin, white stripe all the way around my wrist, and when I touched it, I couldn't feel anything. The skin was completely numb.

Some of the happy feeling went away.

"What did you mean when you said that the monster had gone?" I asked.

"Exactly that. That when I... woke up... then, well, then it was gone."

I found that hard to believe. That it was dead, yes, possibly – I could believe that. Chimera's heart had stopped beating. I knew it. I'd been holding it in my fiery hand when it happened. But the shapeless, bubbling body that had come close to crashing down on us like a wave... something must have happened to it, something must be... left behind.

And sure enough.

I found her not far away, concealed by the tall green grass. She was lying very still on her belly with her hands stretched up above her head and her face turned slightly to one side. She wasn't wearing much in the way of clothes, only a pair of stumpy pyjama bottoms and a tattered, filthy, white T-shirt that was decorated with the black, white and grey silhouettes of birds.

Chimera had turned into Kimmie. And Kimmie had died.

I knelt down beside her. The air kept telling me that everything was fine, that nothing was wrong. But everything was not fine.

It was hard not to feel relief that Chimera had gone. If it had been a dead Chimera figure lying there, with or without wings, then I don't think I would have felt anything but that – good riddance.

But it was Kimmie. Skinny, weary and drained, with frail, pointy bones under her pale, filthy skin. And once upon a time Kimmie had been a little girl who loved birds and had a really bad relationship with her dad.

"Are you crying?" asked Kahla, who'd come to join me.

"No. All right, maybe a little."

Cat sniffed the dead girl in the grass.

"Meowwwwwwrrrrrrrr," he said. What it meant, only he knew. Then he turned around languidly and strode away with his tail pointing straight up.

"Where are you going?" I asked.

Home, he said. *Are you coming?*

"We can't just... leave."

Why not?

I looked helplessly at Kimmie's dead body.

"Because we can't. Surely we have to do... something."

There's nothing to do, Cat said with obvious Cat logic. *Unless you're going to eat it?*

"Oh, stop it..."

But to an animal it was that simple. When something was alive then it was alive. When something died, it was dead and uninteresting, unless it was edible.

"I'm not an animal," I said.

Cat made no reply. He just stepped into his own personal wildways fog and disappeared. Once I'd finished my peculiar human deliberations, I could choose whether or not I wanted to follow.

The grass behind us rustled. Kimmie's dad came walking, upright and on legs that looked a little unsteady, but that seemed to be in working order again. His face was totally devoid of expression, but there was a slight hesitation in his movements. He stopped next to us and looked down at his daughter.

"So she's dead," he said.

I looked at him. I had a strong feeling that the bird T-shirt and the pyjama bottoms were the clothes Kimmie had worn the night he chased her outside and then locked her out because she'd tried to steal food from the kitchen. Did he recognize them? Did he remember? I could see neither sorrow nor remorse in his face. If he felt anything like that, he didn't show it.

"Where's her sister buried?" I asked.

"Maira? In the churchyard, of course."

"Then make sure Kimmie's buried beside her," I said. My voice sounded different. Hoarser and more adult, as if I could actually tell a man like him what to do and expect him to do it. A little like Aunt Isa, perhaps.

His face was still blank. As though he might as well have been stuffed rather than have flesh and blood and a heart inside, but he nodded briefly, once.

"I suppose that's the thing to do," he said.

I still didn't know if he regretted anything or felt the slightest bit guilty. But he knelt down and picked up the girl's body in his arms as if it wasn't a dead thing being transported, but a living girl he was carrying home.

His dead daughter in his arms, he left without saying another word. And without looking back.

CHAPTER TWENTY-FOUR

Home

"...And then he just left without saying anything. And we'd just saved his life."

Kahla was doing most of the talking. I couldn't really find the words. I just sat on Aunt Isa's threadbare sofa with Cat on my lap, trying to look happy and relieved. And so I was. Cat was alive. The badger cubs were being suckled by their mother. And I had a strong hunch that Martin had regained consciousness at the hospital. Hopefully he could now move all of his body, not just his angry head. There was a lot to be grateful for, a lot to be happy about.

Mrs Pommerans sat in the armchair opposite, listening attentively.

"So you chucked the whole tin of vademecum powder into the air in one go," she said.

"Yes."

"Then what happened?"

"Like Kahla said. We fell asleep and dreamt some crazy dreams, and when we woke up... Chimera was dead."

"Yes. But what happened in your 'crazy dreams'? The same as in Kahla's?"

Kahla had only talked about snow and cold and the feeling of turning into ice. I didn't think for one moment that she'd experienced the same as me.

"No, there was... a little more."

I couldn't tell them. The words just wouldn't come, everything seemed stuck inside my head – Chimera, Kimmie, her stuffed dad, Cat and Maira, the fiery hand... How could I tell them so it all made sense?

"You met the hungry one?" Mrs Pommerans guessed, and looked at me over the rim of her spectacles. "Am I right?"

"Yes."

"And you... chased the revenant out of her?"

"I... I think so." How did she know that?

Mrs Pommerans smiled. "Oh, I am pleased."

Perhaps you just knew things like that when you were as old and as skilled a wildwitch as she was.

"So has the soul tangle been untangled?" Aunt Isa asked.

"Oh, yes," Mrs Pommerans said. "Everything is as it should be. Boy is boy, hawk is hawk, and so on.

Clara could do with some practice at Journeying, but we can sort that out later. There's just one thing..."

"What's that?" I said.

"You separated the hunger and the hungry. You set Kimmie free."

"Yes."

"What happened to the revenant?"

I had to think about that.

"I don't know. I... I grabbed it with..." I flapped the hand which had been on fire. "I think I stopped it. But then... everything exploded. And I couldn't see it or Kimmie or... or anything else. I... I guess I woke up. In a forest that was very much alive." I took a sip of my tepid tea. "Aunt Isa... it felt as if the Earth were breathing. Is that possible? As if it were rising and sinking and... breathing out something warm."

"I don't know," Aunt Isa said. "I've never heard of that before."

Mrs Pommerans bit her lip and suddenly looked much younger. Like a schoolgirl who's been caught doing something she shouldn't.

"Agatha," Aunt Isa said. "What is it?"

"Oh," Mrs Pommerans said. "That would explain it."

"Explain what?"

"Why the forest was a little too alive. If someone had chucked a whole tin of vademecum powder over it."

"What do you mean?"

"Fruitful dreams," Mrs Pommerans said. "If you add even a tiny bit to your watering can when you water your plants, then... then you get a very lovely-looking garden. But a whole box... That's probably overdoing it a bit."

Aunt Isa couldn't help laughing.

"Agatha. So that's why your garden is always so warm and green."

"Yes. That's my little secret. Please don't tell anyone."

"I thought you had found a way of manipulating the weather."

"Isa! As if I would! It's strictly forbidden!"

"Hi, Mum."

"Mousie!"

Mum made a real effort not to look too relieved, but she was super pleased to see me safe and sound, there was no doubt about that.

I could have spent a few more days with Aunt Isa; less than a week had passed since Mum picked me up from the hospital. But I fancied going home and being non-wildwitchy for a while. I had a lot on my mind.

"How are you feeling, munchkin? How's your head?"

My head? Oh. The concussion. I'd forgotten all about it. A measly little headache. Not worth worrying about when you were battling soul tangles, revenants and stuffed fathers.

"Fine," I said. "My head doesn't hurt any more."

"Great. Any nausea?"

"Nope. None at all."

"Excellent. Because I was just about to start dinner. Can you lend me a hand or are you too tired?"

I was hungry. I had to double-check, but it was regular great-we're-eating-soon-hunger. Not the kind that made me sniff new-born baby badgers.

"We can do it together. Is it OK if I just call Oscar first?"

"Of course, darling."

I went to my room. There are certain things mums don't need to hear.

"Oscar?"

"Yesss. What's up?"

"It's all good. I... I don't think I need to be scared of turning into a grass snake again. That is unless I choose to."

"Great. So does that mean you've learned to do it on purpose?"

"Pretty much." Mrs Pommerans had given me some exercises as well as a small amount of vade-mecum powder to take home. But not for the pot plants, she had warned me.

"Cool! Please can you show me how it's done?"

"No, not really. Or at least I don't think so. I was just wondering... Have you heard how Martin is?"

"Martin the Meanie?"

"Who else? But..."

"But what?"

"I think we should stop calling him that."

"Why? Just because he fell off a roof? He's out of hospital. He's fine now – some people from his class visited him and they say he'll be back in school on Monday. Just as mean as he always was, no doubt."

I'd been pretty sure that was the case, but it was good to have it confirmed.

"That's not the reason. It's just... Have you ever heard the expression: give a dog a bad name?"

"Explain?"

"That the bad name becomes a self-fulfilling prophecy. Think about The Nothing. And... and what about Mousie?"

"Are you saying that if we start calling him Martin the Sweetie, he'll suddenly become all sweetness and light?" There was disbelief in Oscar's voice, and I couldn't help smiling. It did require a bit of a leap of faith.

"No, maybe not... but we could always try."

"You're out of your mind," he said.

"Likewise."

"Gotta go. Dinner is ready," he said. "See you tomorrow?"

Cat was lying on my tummy. The fluorescent hands on my Mickey Mouse alarm clock were about to meet at the number twelve. It was almost midnight and I was dog-tired and yet I couldn't sleep.

Fruitful dreams, I thought. Because there was one thing I really needed to know. Something I couldn't find in a book or look up on the Internet.

Mrs Pommerans's little tin was sitting next to the alarm clock, but I hesitated. I hadn't forgotten what happened the last time I opened it.

Go to sleep, Cat growled grumpily.

"I can't."

Why not?

"Because I'm thinking about Kimmie."

She's fine.

"What do you mean?" I killed her, I thought, but didn't say it out loud. "She's dead!"

Yes. So she's fine.

Seriously, cats.

You'll pay for this. Those were the words Chimera had screamed at me when I took her wings, and she'd said them again in the grey snow world. There's a price. You *will* pay for this.

She'd been right. There was a price to pay. And although it definitely wasn't what she'd had in mind when she said it, Chimera's greatest revenge was that for the rest of my life I would carry with me the knowledge that I had killed her. That was the price: my mind would never be free from the image of dead Kimmie – so small, so skinny, in her filthy bird T-shirt with bare legs sticking out of her pyjama bottoms.

I reached out for the small, silver tin. Opened it carefully. Dabbed a tiny, tiny amount on my forefinger and brushed it between my eyebrows where the scars from Cat's claws were still visible. Then I carefully closed the tin and lay down.

Nothing happened. Nothing except that I finally started feeling a little drowsy. I yawned.

Then it came. Only a very brief glimpse.

I was in the living forest. Two girls were walking in front of me, holding hands. One had a jackdaw on her shoulder.

There was nothing more. Nothing but that. And yet my sense of relief was so great I thought I could fly. I would never forget Kimmie, but nor would her memory weigh as heavily as I'd feared.

"She's fine," I said.

Of course, Cat growled and yawned. *I told you so, didn't I?*

NEXT IN THE WILDWITCH SERIES

PUSHKIN CHILDREN'S BOOKS

We created Pushkin Children's Books to share tales from different languages and cultures with younger readers, and to open the door to the wide, colourful worlds these stories offer.

From picture books and adventure stories to fairy tales and classics, and from fifty-year-old bestsellers to current huge successes abroad, the books on the Pushkin Children's list reflect the very best stories from around the world, for our most discerning readers of all: children.